WARLOCK

BOOKS BY JIM HARRISON

Novels
WOLF
A GOOD DAY TO DIE
FARMER
LEGENDS OF THE FALL
WARLOCK

Poetry
PLAIN SONG
LOCATIONS
OUTLYER
LETTERS TO YESENIN
RETURNING TO EARTH

JIM HARRISON
WARLOCK

DELACORTE PRESS/SEYMOUR LAWRENCE

AF

Published by
Delacorte Press/Seymour Lawrence
1 Dag Hammarskjold Plaza
New York, N.Y. 10017

The lines from "The Men That Don't Fit In" from THE
COLLECTED POEMS OF ROBERT SERVICE are reprinted by
permission of Dodd, Mead and Company, Inc., McGraw-Hill Ryerson
Limited and Ernest Benn Limited.

Manufactured in the United States of America

First printing

Designed by MaryJane DiMassi

LIBRARY OF CONGRESS CATALOGING IN PUBLICATION DATA

Harrison, Jim, 1937–
Warlock.

I. Title.
PS3558.A67W37   813'.54   81–9796
ISBN 0–440–09462–3   AACR2
ISBN 0–440–09467–4 (Signed and limited edition)

TO BOB DATTILA

PART ONE

_...I_ _have had a most rare vision. I have had a_
dream, past the wit of man to say what dream
it was: man is but an ass, if he go about to expound this
dream. . . . The eye of man hath not heard, the ear of
man hath not seen, man's hand is not able to taste, his
tongue to conceive, nor his heart to report, what my
dream was.
. . . It shall be called "Bottom's Dream," because it
hath no bottom; and I will sing it in the latter end of
a play . . . to make the more gracious, I shall sing it at
her death.

WM. SHAKESPEARE
A Midsummer-Night's Dream
act 4, scene 1

1

Seven years came and went. But then we seem always in a state of getting ready for something that never quite occurs. *Are you sleeping, are you sleeping, brother John, brother John? O mother brother sister father time:* sidereal time, time for a drink, time for dinner, to get up, sit down, time for grace, time to make love, for zippers and the lifting of skirts: the baby emerged December 11, 1937, at 12:11:37 A.M., the same time that a piece of meteorite killed an elephant in distant Tanzania, Hitler brushed his teeth with some vigor, Einstein yawned.

It is very difficult to be awakened by a phone call with a severe hangover and discover someone you love is dead, especially if that someone is you. Of course it was a dream call but Johnny didn't know that. He stepped out of bed with an extraordinary sense of lightness—so the diet is finally paying off—fairly floating through the dining room to the kitchen where the phone suddenly stopped. And there he was, smack dab in the middle of the kitchen floor; his face looked like where the deep purple fell, a huge windfall plum on the yellow linoleum. Then he was floating back to the bedroom where he screeched with truly hideous volume, and shook his wife, Diana, awake.

"I'm out there and I'm dead. I'm dead."

"But you're here, darling." She rose to her knees in alarm, the sheet falling from her shoulder.

"I'm in the kitchen and I'm dead," he sobbed, slamming his head into her lap with rigid force. "On the floor, dead as a doornail, for god's sake. Go look."

"This better not be some chintzy way of getting laid." But no, his shoulders were shaking uncontrollably. She scrambled down the bed, after shoving him away like a piece of cordwood. For the first time in their seven years of marriage he did not stare at her beautiful bottom—oh gates of hell—when she got out of bed. And it wasn't that this particular bottom was framed by a foreshortened, satin slip nightie gotten mail order from Los Angeles; no, it was simply one of the best on earth, way up in that realm where comparisons are truly odious. She returned from the body search. "There's nothing on the kitchen floor but the tipped over garbage can. I think it fair to presume the garbage can isn't you. Now I have two hours to sleep before I go to work."

"It must have been a dream," he said, with precarious certainty. He poked tentatively at her bottom which, he felt, had a curious way of aiming at him, somewhat in the manner that those at the bottom of the genetic pool feel that TV performers are talking to them.

"Oh god, darling, not now. I'll do anything after work. Just let me sleep."

"Anything?" he chuckled, getting up. "I'll make you a dinner you won't forget. Fish, game, fowl, veal, pork? Throw a dart at the culinary map, baby, and it'll be on the table." He really wasn't so much a fool as he was giddy about still being alive.

"Please be quiet, darling."

He dressed quickly and smacked Hudley, the dog, for the garbage can mess, a ritual repeated countless times. Why would a dog want the forbidden fruit of leftover sauerkraut?

It was only a little after five A.M. and barely light; dawn in June comes early in northern climes for reasons which a reader might check in an encyclopedia (Johnny himself owned the fourteenth edition of the Britannica, published in 1929, in order to avoid all those chilling photos of jet fighters, and mockups of atoms falling apart with disastrous consequences). He drove down to Lake Michigan, only a few miles from any farmhouse on the hilly Leelanau Peninsula. It was one of those rare lambent, umbrous mornings when the still warm air was full of green haze, and presented the illusion that one lived in a fairy tale, and everything would work out. Somewhere on this beach, he thought, Rapunzel might lie in wait in a pup tent. The dog was head deep in the water; his preferred method of drinking was merely to open his mouth and let the water run in. Johnny tried to remember when he had last been up at dawn without staying up all night. To be frank, he couldn't, and it occurred to him it might be time at his age, forty-two, to start turning back the old Big Ben alarm. It was the only chance in a frenetic world to see the true serenity of earth, he thought. There was the troublesome idea that Lake Michigan should somehow look bigger, though you couldn't see across it, and it stretched nearly four hundred miles from Chicago to so far north that Chicago was easily forgotten; and the water was so pure and clear it might remind the natives of the north of the Bahamas had they ever been there, which they hadn't. The thought clarified itself when he remembered that the Pacific looked much larger than the Atlantic. Then the dream came back with such force that he looked around wildly for company to convince himself he had returned from the dreamworld: Hudley streaked past, chasing a flock of flying gulls with comforting awkwardness.

Less than a dozen miles out in the lake which was uncommonly dulcet, housebroken, not altogether a suitable stage for his death dream, were the Manitou Islands; the sacred home for the great spirit, he had heard, but didn't know the particulars. Even the local hippies scorned the poor indigenous Indians as being less interesting than those of the Rockies; but then the alternative life-style types in Leelanau County had pretty much traded in their turquoise jewelry in favor of the wood stove revolution. His only real connection with the American Indian was his secret name, given him thirty years ago as a cub scout when he was inducted into the sacred order of the Webelos. The scoutmaster, who was also the school bandleader, was a trifle fey and liked the idea of giving this morose youngster, the son of the local police chief, a name that would doom him to the far side of heaven. Warlock. From that day on in the privacy of his own thought he was Warlock. Not a year later the scoutmaster had been run out of town after having been discovered in the middle of a sodomic frenzy in a camp privy.

He realized that, in that he was facing west, there was no point waiting around for the sunrise. He tossed the big dog in the back of the Subaru, and drove eastward across the peninsula, squinting at the rising sun as he passed through the village of Lake Leelanau. His favorite local place, the grocery store, wouldn't be open for another hour or so. He was breathing deeply now, far from his plum-faced death, and heading home —there was an off chance Diana might have time for an embrace or two. Then he noticed a new road with a sudden sense of shock. Impossible! In the year of temporary unemployment, he had covered every road on the official county map. Now they were springing a new one on him.

The road had been hidden by a triangle of trees, and what he had thought of as a double driveway. And the road had the courtesy to own a sign that read Dead End: no wonder he hadn't bothered with it. He drove a few hundred yards, ending up in the yard of a deserted, vandalized farmhouse. He got out, allowing Hudley to run interference, in a thicket of green burdocks, noting that he could see right through the empty windows to the Manitou Islands out in Lake Michigan. Glorious. He walked around the house and framed the red sun in another empty window. Always the art critic, he ascribed a definite "interesting" to these ruins.

Back home he was disappointed to find Diana in a rush to get ready for work. He drank a glass of ice water as she stood in her undies by the coffee maker which they had brought, at his insistence, because of a Joe DiMaggio commercial.

"How about a quicky?" he said, following her to the bedroom where she slipped on her nurse's uniform.

"No time, darling. Would you mind cooking something simple tonight? Say, with a light hand on the spice rack?"

"Jeezo. Here I sit, unfucked and my cooking criticized. High and dry. Do you have time to tuck me in?" he added archly.

"If you hurry." She tapped her foot as he ripped off his clothes. She had been the sole daughter in a family that included four brothers and had a profound understanding of men. She arranged the sheet around his neck as a barber would, and kissed his brow. He was a world-class sleeper and was already drifting off as she brushed her golden hair. She noted that his brow was beginning to furrow. His spicy cooking and absurd nightmare had scarcely provided her with the sort of sleep a surgical nurse needs. The poor soul has just figured out he's going to die someday, she thought, leaving for work.

She was right on the money because she was very smart. Johnny was, in fact, taking dictation in his dreams: one of those curious, relatively rare dreams where there is a voice, and the voice presumes to give instructions. He was commanded to change his future. The summer before, his ninety-six-year-old grandmother had told him of such a voice: first she heard a soprano singing a hymn in Swedish, then a huge rushing of a river, then the voice, "Don't ever go back to Milwaukee. There's mud on the streets in Milwaukee." In her dreams Johnny had recognized the roots of prophecy. If a faddish contemporary evangelist, say Oral Roberts, had such a dream, Johnny thought, Milwaukee would be in for trouble in regards to tourism. But to change the future moment by moment. To throw this fatal gauntlet in the snout of life. Deep in his dreams he became a cowboy, a fireman, a farmer, a sailor at the prow of a barkentine sailing across a coal black sea. The dream was a violent baptism, a little vitiated by the detail, just before awakening, of Johnny receiving a blowjob from a crone in Spain. Her face looked like a shucked pecan. But the voice itself was an oracular baritone and came from a water-filled puddle where a tree had tipped over.

2

The trouble is that nobody gets to be anyone else. The often sorry mental states of actors and actresses attest to that. Meet them. See the folly whirling in their eyes.

At breakfast, really lunch, John Lundgren-Warlock meditated on his new life over a plate of leftover hasenpfeffer—a German-style marinated rabbit stew. Diana hadn't liked it the evening before. As a neophyte cook he had a heavy hand with the spices, not comprehending how easily more can become less. Now he doodled with his laden plate, poking here and there so that each strand of egg noodle might absorb its dark freight of sauce. He had absentmindedly added a half dozen cloves of garlic late in the cooking and had been forced to admit to Diana that the taste was a tad raw. But powerful, he insisted.

"Why don't you simply bite your fucking tongue," she said.

"Sorry, darling. My first time out of the chute with the recipe."

"I'm sorry, too. We lost one today."

"How old?"

"Your age. But terribly fat. It was ghastly pumping at those fat, hairy breasts." At forty-two his interest in mortality statistics had increased. Milestones in *Time* magazine had become more poignant.

"If you don't mind," he said, gesturing at his diminishing plate. She had pushed hers away and lit a Vantage Ultra light.

"Then he let go all over the bed. Number two, to be exact. He had been in a pizza eating contest the night before. He weighed over three hundred. Drove a UPS truck. Left a wife and two little children sitting out in the hall reading horror comics."

"Diana!" He continued eating, now without relish.

"You told me to unwind after work."

Now working over the leftovers, he reflected on how as an emergency and cardiac nurse Diana was certainly out there on the firing line. Still charged with his partly waking dream he wondered how much of his new life he could share with her. Diana tended toward the acerbic, the caustic, and it might make sense to keep this new baptism secret until it panned out. He lowered the food to the dog, Hudley, a rather massive Airedale. The dog, after one tentative lap, rejected the hasenpfeffer. Hudley had never refused food before, not even an experimental leaf of lettuce, or a cracker with Tabasco for punishment. He pretended that the cracker wasn't hot. Lundgren-Warlock had bought the dog as a pup after reading a dog article that described *Le feu d'Airedaile*—the Airedale fire. Now the best that could be said was that the dog was an individual. Early in his puberty Hudley had developed an affection for garbage cans as sexual objects. The dog would push a can over and hump it in a hypnotic frenzy. Diana would say, quite the dog you bought, buster. She was a farm girl and didn't

believe in house dogs. She punished Hudley, justly and unmercifully, while Warlock heaped love on the dog as some sort of
obtuse soul mate. Quite naturally the dog adored Diana and
only tolerated Warlock, unless he was being fed or taken for
a ride. For better and usually worse, Hudley was his Rozinante,
though without saddle and snaffle. On a whim he went to the
refrigerator and put a handful of grated cheese on the leftovers.
Hudley loved cheese. No dice. The dog growled, then abruptly
went to sleep in a pool of sun coming through the window.

So much for cuisine, back to the future, he thought. Plans.
Take a shower. Examine moments and how they might be
radicalized. A mere fruit fly alters the taste of a glass of wine.
Specific plans. I have the unemployment office. What's for
dinner? Something subtle in lieu of the rabbit vinaigrette. The
Indians and their power food. Hop to the shower like a great
big bunny.

In truth Lundgren-Warlock owned a few loose ends, ends
that would come clear to an apt reader of resumés. Resumés
tell the real story, assuming you are an engine, a boat, a building. Two marriages of seven years apiece: the first a cauldron
of grief and pleasure that ended when at thirty-two he had
proposed to Diana at a county fair. The pursuit was successful,
though later when he played her Bob Dylan's mournful song
about a girl at a north country fair she heehawed, being without
sentiment over the lyrics of popular music. Only a few nights
before as he scanned the new *Playboy* for good articles and
beaver shots at the kitchen table, he could hear her singing
along with Handel's *Messiah*.

Standing in the bathroom after a shower that was not quite
right, he wiped steam from the lower part of the mirror in order
to see his dick. There it is. Then it disappeared as the steam

reinvaded. Just checking it out. The body wasn't too bad considering a neglect of weight. He was five eleven and three quarters and weighed about two hundred. Years before, the Air Force had refused to round off the fraction to the nearest whole number and he had been forced to lose ten pounds. He had gone from the steam tables of college dormitories to the steam tables of the Air Force, wanting to be a pilot but narrowly flunking the physical—a slight stigma in the right eye.

While dressing he closed his eyes to recapture the power of his dream of the future, the green unwinding of the morning drive, with the lake a heartless aquamarine beckoning with a signed promise of new life. He stumbled backward on the bed. Not that he was a dope, a schlepp as they say. He didn't care about that sort of thing, and often went quite contrary to fashion in dress and behavior. In college his econ major had been liberally strewn with courses in philosophy and literature and psychology. He had been thought quite the wise one among his cronies and was given to quipping "Tell it to Anne Frank" to those who whined about life's difficulties.

As an instance, several nights before, he and Diana had watched Tom Snyder after an energetic bout of making love; an attractive woman, Nancy Friday, had told Tom that eighty-five percent of all women surveyed said they defined masculinity in terms of whether or not a man was a good provider. Diana had been uncommonly tender, taking his hand.

"Don't be upset."

"I'm not."

"You'll find something. Just don't get depressed. They must have all been brainless cunts."

"That's okay, darling. Not to be corny but I've always tried to do it my way."

"That's terribly corny. You should stop listening to the radio."

"I'm interested in the news. In the world beyond our petty interests."

"Oh God. You could always paint portraits again."

"Nope. Shut up."

They had wrangled themselves into a grand screw on the floor, the dog growling in the middle distance.

3

Warlock was pissed. His first wife, Marilyn, used to say "Define your anger." She was given to the more otiose forms of psychologizing. During a particularly bad period of their marriage she had insisted that they had never really "learned how to touch," no matter that their mutual sexual athleticism had far surpassed that imagined by the best directors of pornographic films. She would advance on him, hips ajar, as if she were Clint Eastwood and her tiny clitoris a .44 Magnum.

The future would be his own, goddammit! He had lost a precious year struggling with negativism, with self-criticism, just because there had been no place for him among the fungi of the Traverse City business community. He had been whirling like a self-righting sailboat in a bottomless ocean, never upright for more than a few moments. The vertiginous plunge from forty-five thousand a year as a foundation executive to the dole had nipped his life in the fatigued bud. The dream was a new start, a break in reality, glittering sunlight after a sodden, endless summer storm.

He opened a can of dog food with abandon, twisting the can

opener with a new vigor. The dog approached with his accustomed low, guttural growl.

"Shut up Hudley you stupid motherfucker!" he yelled. The dog sat down, utterly startled. Warlock grabbed it, hoisting the dog's ninety pounds to his shoulder level. "You fucking growl at me again and I'm pitching your dead ass in front of a truck. Get it? Get it?" He dropped the dog to the floor. Hudley nibbled at his food with a worried expression, stunned at this unexampled behavior and having no real notion what had caused it.

Warlock stepped out onto the back porch, breathing deeply to control the adrenaline rush. After a moment the dog scratched at the screen. On the porch Hudley leaned against his leg, wagging his tail. Fascism was evidently effective with dogs, he thought. He felt the clarity of having done something differently. Maybe the opportunity would arise again soon, he hoped. Meanwhile there was the problem of what to fix for dinner. On a whim he had bought five pounds of frozen squid for the amazingly low price of seventy-five cents a pound. But he had never eaten squid, let alone prepared it, and he wondered if this might provide a minimal adventure of sorts. His anger had offered up a sharp tinge of lust and he pondered the short-term effects of masturbation. It could be a disastrously energy-stealing act, making a good squid dinner unlikely. Once in New York a few years before, he had masturbated in his hotel after a bad landing at La Guardia and slept through an important meeting with the Ford Foundation. He had apologized, inventing a severe attack of colitis after a near plane crash as an excuse, but it had been nerve wracking to imagine that those imposing Ford Foundation executives might somehow know that he had been jerking off over Miss April, who had expressed interest in wind-surfing, gothic novels, and intellectual men.

No, pulling the pud would be counterproductive; the frozen squid demanded his attention and wit. The roasted chicken of the night before last had been less than successful, and he recognized it might be time to subdue his creative impulses in favor of recipe books. The chicken itself had been succulent but the oyster stuffing, which reflected his originality, had poured out when he tilted the platter, with a certain sense of the fecal. There was more to oyster stuffing evidently than a can of frozen oysters and their pearlish liquid.

"Oh my god," Diana had said.

"Hmm, not real cute."

"It might be good. I'll shut my eyes."

"That's not funny. Something doesn't have to be beautiful to taste good."

"Sorry. Give me a leg, a thigh, you can have all of the stew."

"You're trying the stuffing, goddammit."

"Nothing doing, mother. The chicken's not bad. A little dry but not really bad. You were thinking about sex."

"B.F.D., Sherlock, how do you know?"

"Your mouth always opens and your tongue probes the air like a big fat snake in a swamp. I bet it wasn't me on your mind."

"I'm not particularly fat. Maybe ten pounds over."

"Twenty by the charts. Let's hope it wasn't you know who? Miss South of the Border."

Isabella had proven a sore point when, after a cocktail party a half dozen years ago, he had confessed his infidelity to Diana. She'd held him as he wept, forgiving him after her initial

sorrow. The drama of the moment had been increased somewhat by a confession of her own. Shortly after her college
graduation when Warlock had thought of them as sort-of-
engaged, she had gone to Chicago to have a model portfolio
made by a prominent photographer, a trip financed by her
father, who thought of her as the most beautiful little girl in
the whole wide world. As Johnny's tears dried she admitted the
photographer had taken advantage of her, and so great was her
shock she was unable to resist. Warlock had stomped around
the room, then, in a jealous rage.

"You mean he just plumb stuck it in? No foreplay when you
could have run for it?"

"No, silly. My eyes were closed. I was supposed to be sleeping or something and he caught me by surprise."

"I don't get it."

"The grim details are he simply stuck his tongue in and it
went on from there."

"That's always been your weakness, but you could have torn
his hair out. Was he real big?"

"Not terribly. About average. Nearly everyone is average."

"What's your basis of comparison, Miss Promiscuity?"

"None of your beeswax. I'm not an acre of your property.
Was I supposed to keep chaste in anticipation of marrying you
someday? And stop stomping around like you're the champ
fuck of the world, you Hitler bastard."

As nasty as the evening was it was followed by a week of truly
magnificent sex, finally ended by her period. Warlock at heart
was a finicky Calvinist in those days. He had controlled his urge
to toss the whole mess in her face. Tears of rage had formed,
checked only by a flash of his dream which froze the whole
tableau of dinner. Had the blowjob in Seville at the end of the

dream really been in Seville after all? The slightly fermented scent of cooked oysters threw him back to a moonlit night in Corona with a fair breeze coming off Flushing Bay, and a file clerk named Isabella whose dark Spanish looks (Puerto Rican) had dazzled him in a foundation office. He had passed his hotel number to her, and, her curiosity sufficiently piqued, they had had dinner and drinks, ending up on a mattress on the roof of her apartment building in Corona. What a magical night it had been, with her cousin's record player in the apartment below them playing foreign songs of love and torment.

Diana waved a chicken leg across his field of vision and he returned to the table with a slight blush.

"I was thinking about my job. My old job."

4

There were three sisters playing in Lake Michigan beyond a long glistening blond sandspit—they wore green one-piece bathing suits, drawn, in the new fashion, well up their thighs. He had no proof that they were sisters, or that they were thirteen, fourteen and fifteen. He owned an imponderable urge to both create and consume low-rent information, an urge balanced by his superbly inaccurate observations. Were he a writer, he would have been working on a History of Rain.

The three sisters continued playing unmindful of his thought, something that he noted happened all the time. Play on, girls! They chose this moment to swivel against a small wave and simultaneously stare at him. He waved as the one on the far left rearranged the bottoms of her suit, which had pulled up a bit into the crack of her buttocks with a delightful effect.

It was after five and the beach was vacant except for the four of them. He had driven Diana to work with a special intensity, however phony, his Hermes briefcase between them signifying a more prosperous time. After work she was having a quick supper, then on to her ERA meeting, a group which she led with grace and intelligence. She was one of those farm girl valedictorians who go through college and into life with the confidence of gaited horses. She was the only daughter among three sons and, as the apple of her father's eye, had been raised with a quantum of parental and male esteem. Such women, Warlock had read in *Ladies' Home Journal,* are usually multi-orgasmic and have a definite edge in marital and public life. At thirty-two she was without a cavity and had only recently confessed to him an IQ superior to his own, after repeated questioning. He had suddenly felt dumb. Oh for a fat pay-check.

He tapped at the briefcase, then slid his hand up her resplendently white nurse's uniform. Why wouldn't she return to garter belts and the half foot of bare thigh? They often drove with his hand snuggling toward bull's-eye but the habit was mitigated a great deal by the advent of panty hose. His little finger poked tentatively upward.

"Stop it. I don't want to get all worked up."

"Sorry. I was absentminded."

"Bullshit. You should have gotten up earlier when there was still time."

"I feel the torpor of the unemployed."

"You read that in the paper yesterday. I read it myself. Stop getting your feelings out of the newspaper."

"You're right. An hour with the paper is a dead pecker shot. Remember when it only took fifteen minutes?"

"Stop remembering anything. It's not doing you any good."

"Is this a hint of your Oriental leanings?"

"For god's sake, Johnny. I just want you to get your spine back and be happy."

"Thanks. Don't worry. I got a plan."

The plan that day was the beach, but only the beach in lieu of voluminous clouds of mosquitoes that infest Michigan in June. Stragglers in the forest have actually died in torment from these insects. He needed the sense of wilderness, but not death threats if he strayed from well worn paths. Diana was so right about newspapers and the little death of wasted time. The sole memorable item recently had been the disappearance of a honeymooning Brazilian couple. The account had said they had been out for a walk and had broken through the earth where the crust was especially thin, and fallen into an underground river. He had never wanted to go to South America in the first place. And more important, the beach rekindled his memories of the great Gauguin.

The failure of his own art career was a grief too deep and raw for Warlock to recognize. At his mother's instigation he had won a boy scout's merit badge in art. That got him started at thirteen and by the time he reached college he was a more than passable portraitist. In fact this talent put him through college: there were countless renderings of rich wives, businessmen, politicians, children. His Phi Delt fraternity brothers frequently put him to work doing nudes. They were a happy spermatic group, always in need of new material for their jerkoff marathons. He had even, out of kindness, painted a small male nude for the one bad apple in the house, a diminutive homo from Kalamazoo. Lucky for the homo that he was rich, as that excuses all behavior for those who envy the condition.

His heart swelled at the beach. If only Gauguin had been his brother. If only Gauguin had been Warlock, or vice versa. What pride and strength and grace and energy. But his mother had died of complications of muscular dystrophy when he was a senior in high school and she had been the backbone of his art aspirations. His father, who was currently near retirement and the top detective in Minneapolis, had urged him vehemently toward more practical pursuits. The ever-changing soul of the water drew him back to Gauguin. The great Gauguin would have had the girls back in his studio in a trice. In the summer of his twenty-second year, in 1960 to be exact, he had taken a portfolio of his original paintings to New York, along with a few portraits. He went by Greyhound and during a rest stop in Pittsburgh, had rather shyly drawn a beret from his valise. The life of Art! Blue water! His other great yearning had been to be in the Navy in the Pacific during World War II with his father and uncles. His father had shaken hands with General Douglas MacArthur and had had the photo to prove it.

One of the girls in green approached, the loose sand forcing a wonderful flex in her legs, with just a tad of furze at the edge of her crotch as if there just might be a half a peach in there struggling with itself. His throat swelled just short of closing.

"Got a ciggy, please?"

"Sure thing. Only Ultra lights. Watching my health."

"My ciggies got wet. We had a joint and it got wet, too."

"Sorry, but I don't have a joint. Used to smoke pot in the old days."

"Why'd you stop?" She inhaled deeply and squatted down a few feet from his face.

"Not sure. It seemed to steal my incentive." He was in an utter dither. She smelled like the sun.

"Fuck the incentive. I like to get stoned."

"You're very pretty."

"So?"

"So nothing. It was just a compliment."

"So next time bring a joint and we might make music." She winked and strutted off.

She would be wonderful if she talked like Audrey Hepburn, he thought. Not that he would have kicked her out of the sack for eating crackers.

5

When he got home he lay down on the bed, frazzled by the sun, and had a reverie about his first art conquest in New York twenty years before:

She took off her bathrobe. Nothing unusual he thought. She sat on the couch beside him and he slumped until his head rested against her knee. She owned the same bullfight poster that he had tacked to his wall but that didn't depress him. Like minds. She somehow smelled pink. She gently lifted the beret from his head and parted her legs a bit so that his face nestled between her knees.

"You're just another crazy artist."

"You might say that."

"I always wanted to be a bohemian but I guess I just didn't have the guts."

He peered at her pubis and navel, thinking oddly of the word guts. She obviously had them, verging, as she did, a little over the line of plumpness but not unpleasantly.

"I guess I figured it was my destiny. I mean art."

She parted her legs even further so that it was with a certain strain that he supported his head, a burdensome size eight.

"I guess we're beating around the bush," she said. "What's your favorite thing sexwise?"

"I like it all." He sat up and began taking off his shirt.

"You might say I'm orally directed. Give and take. You know?"

"I think I catch on."

He did an awkward little dance removing his shoes, pants and underpants. She lunged forward, yanking at his part as if to start an outboard motor. If only the great Gauguin could see him now. She seemed to take aim with her head, engulfing his penis with a single thrust of her mouth. This was not the collegiate nibbling expedition that he was accustomed to. This was New York. This was Greenwich Village. She drew him down on the couch, an implacable chewing magnet, throwing a graceful thigh over his head. He made a slight attempt to slow her down when the pounding seemed as though it might seriously bruise his lips.

During a lull they dressed and went out to an Italian restaurant around the corner from Bleecker. It had a redolent charm, consisting of red-and-white checked tablecloths, candles in old Chianti bottles, and oddly, he thought, the same Manolete bullfight poster. They were flushed and hungry and he thought it witty of her when she clicked his glass.

"Wine is the food of love."

He looked into her hazel eyes as deeply as he could. In a way, he thought, she was a Valkyrie.

"I never knew love could be like that."

"I tried to do my best for you, Johnny." She took his hand and kissed it.

The pasta turned out to be a bit sticky and glutinous, but the marinara sauce laced with chunks of sausage was delicious. He loved the vulgar bite of garlic, a spice never known in his parents' house and for that matter rarely used in the heartland in those days. There was a vaguely sour note when she wouldn't let him have his cup of coffee after dinner.

"I said wine is the food of love. Not coffee. Coffee and sex are enemies."

"Who says?"

"My experience talks loud. Coffee is antilife. Trust me, Johnny. Please."

"We can't exactly go on like that all the time."

"Johnny, limits are set by man not God. How do you know what you can do? Maybe you can fuck like a Greek god all night."

"Maybe you got a point." He was flustered by a woman saying fuck.

"Few of us know our potentials," she went on. "Fewer still know our sexual potentials. And fewer yet develop their sex skills. Sure, men learn football, baseball and what have you, but what about sex?"

His mind blurred, thinking of practicing sex in the manner of a high school football workout. Lundgren, the coach might say, you're going to learn how to be a first rate pussy-eater or you're off the team. Now get down there and go at it like a real man. Put your balls into it. Put your weight into it. Put your heart into it. Put your life into it.

After another extended session he discovered in the shrill light of her bathroom that his dickie was losing its hide. There were rawish splotches. Must he continue injured, as it were? She had even put it in her hinder, a variation that he had only heard of in jokes and locker room talk. There was a definite hankering for sleep.

She sat nude in the kitchen with a largish glass of the food of love. He drank water, then two shots of whiskey. They both sighed deeply, she for more, he for the bed and a book.

"You might be curious about my personal philosophy." She brushed her damp hair back. "I've got idiosyncrasies. For instance I'm from Pennsylvania. I've been here five years and most take me for a native. Nope. I'm from Philadelphia. I learned keypunch operating and I've worked hard. You didn't know I was married once?"

"No. I didn't even guess at it."

"Sad but true. The Korean War took him. I am thirty-five but I don't look it, do I?"

"No. I don't know. I'm no good at ages. I go for the person, not the age."

"That's nice. Bob was that way with me and me with him. He was older but suave, and those goddamn gooks killed him. Killed him." She began to cry and he moved to comfort her. "No matter now. In a way, when I fuck you I fuck Bob. Men are man. You get what I mean?"

"Not actually." He felt flustered and dumb.

"Well, I happen to have a personal philosophy that's not quite ready to reveal to the man on the street. To me, a lot of , the dead aren't really dead. They're what I call the undead. Bob comes back to me in different ways. How do I know he's not you? Can you prove you're not Bob?"

"Nope. I guess I can't."

"Well, even your dicks are the same size though Bob had blue eyes. Yours is a little thicker. But I believe in the power of love and when we buried Bob over at his parents' in Altoona I knew he wasn't really gone. Once he even came to me in the form of a Negro. I can admit it to you because you're artistic and won't be criticizing."

He hugged her, suffused with all the strange griefs of the world. She rose and plopped her trunk on the formica table, wagging her plump bottom at him.

"Let's do it once more? Then you go. I got to get up for work in the morning."

He felt that there was something extremely graceful about her, however sad, something oceanic, utterly lifelike. He stopped at Riker's on Sheridan Square and had poached eggs and two cups of antisex. He vowed to do a portrait of her Rubescence, lolling on black velvet. Walking down Grove Street to his humble quarters, his weenie chafed and twinged rawly against his trousers. He felt it was a hurt that stood for life itself.

6

He emerged from the reverie facing the frozen squid in the sink. How is it possible to feel this stupid at forty-two? He didn't know anything about squid except that they came from the ocean and it was unlikely that the squid would come back to life, under the stream of fresh Michigan water. One thawed enough on the corner for it to be detached. The small tentacles swung limply from the body. The dog stood eagerly beside him so he tickled the dog's nose with the tentacles of the little creature.

"Lucky for you, Hudley, that this fucker isn't twenty foot long."

The dog gobbled, then choked and spit up. In the middle of the squid there was a plasticlike filament of some sort. The squid was beginning to seem less than the perfect buy.

He poured an overlarge goblet of red table wine and sat down at the table with a modest stack of cookbooks before him, but none of their paltry indexes included squid or their alias, cuttlefish. The dream was now offering up a banal polarity of the bad following the good. The suggestion of clarity and power and grace left him feeling stupid when it had diffused. Major moves had to be made and the usual major moves in a man's life involve his job. Of which he had none. Since he lacked a living mother, his aunt had framed his B.S. and M.B.A. degrees as a Christmas gift. They were tucked in the upper shelf of a closet next to a stack of his favorite issues of *Oui, Penthouse* and *Playboy.* He eschewed the hardcore. There was also a barely used vibrator-dildo that Diana considered absurd. He suspected that only a few feet of the old slide down a banister would be sufficient to push her into a frenzy. He knocked on a wood dresser for good luck.

He remembered with a tinge the sheer busyness of selling computer hardware in the Midwest for Burroughs: the rushed lunches and conferences at airports as far flung as Dayton, Cleveland, Detroit, Chicago, Flint; the excited bull sessions with other young salesmen that tapered off after a few years passed. Then the sudden upward move of administering a medium sized family foundation. Marilyn had liked that though her father, a stockbroker from Bloomfield Hills, had recommended he stick with computer hardware. He was proven right in a loathsome way when the IRS began cracking down on family foundations as elaborate tax dodges. By then his first marriage was a sulfurous fumarole and he had given his paper "The Plight of Foundations" to the Spartan Economics Club. Diana was there with a smart-ass senior whose questions led to an after the meeting beer at a student boîte. Their future was sealed (when the boyfriend had gone to pee) with long breathless stares, a classic case of love at first sight—and an equally classic messy aftermath.

The sink was still running. He returned to the kitchen to find that he had inadvertently turned on the warm water and now had a partially poached five pound glob returning his loveless stare from the sink, the squid eyes clouded and deliquescent.

His breath was constricted and on a sudden impulse he ran to the bedroom, grabbed his dirty magazines, the dildo, and the accusatory diplomas. He ran back through the kitchen and out the back door with Hudley following at full bark. He threw everything in the trash barrel and grabbed the charcoal lighter off the grill cover, dumping most of its contents on the magazines. A fulsome roar of orange flame followed the match. The dog raced barking in ever tightening circles around the smut pyre. Warlock stepped back amazed at the heat as if, he thought, the inflamed beavers were protesting. He turned his back and squinted at the sun, a little surprised to see it.

He sensed a new timbre in his voice when he called an old friend in New York, a poet-sculptor, painter, bon vivant, swindler of sorts. Ralph Garth would know what to do with the squid. Warlock wanted to move on from the squid which, since the magazine burning, had lost drama. His foundation which had owned the avowed intent of boosting the Arts and Sciences had given Ralph an ample year's grant to free him from financial worry so that he could devote himself, whole hog, to his work. Warlock and Diana had spent a joyous week with Ralph Garth in New York celebrating the artist's good fortune. Unfortunately the trustees were underwhelmed by the results. One, a huge painted plaster contraption called *The New Leda,* showed an enormous red-dicked swan putting the blocks to a cheerleader who bore more than vague resemblance to Diana. When plugged in the machine went through the motions, as it were, with Ralph Garth there in a railroad engineer's cap, and a can to oil the flanges. The whole project had been at least partially redeemed when NASA with its Arts in Space project cofunded Ralph's attempt to project the avant-garde film *Flaming Creatures* into outer space. There had been a dinner with the governor's wife, an arts patron, a NASA official (who was gay, it turned out), a college president, and other chichi riffraff. Then on a cool autumn night behind the mansion of a trustee, Ralph had projected the film into the heavens in a cylinder of light, somewhat in the fashion that a child shines his flashlight at the moon. Everyone clapped. Warlock had nixed a predinner showing of the film when he learned that an actress-actor transvestite ate a plate of poodle shit in the film. A bit rich for the audience, he judged, after Diana queried Ralph on why anyone would eat poodle shit, and Ralph had replied that there are more things than are dreamt in your philosophy, Horatia. Ralph later admitted he'd netted a cool ten grand after projector and film rental, enabling him to winter in Osso Buco or some such Jamaican hotspot.

"Ralph? This is Warlock. Johnny."

"Oh. Johnny, who's Warlock?"

"An alter ego. Before I forget, I got some squid. How do I cook them?"

"If they're not fresh throw them at passing Negroes." Ralph tended to be cavalier about blacks claiming that a group of them had raped his sister. With minor detective work Warlock had found out that the sister was mythical.

"There're no Negroes up here, Ralph, you know that. And no fresh squid."

"Oh god. Bring them to room temperature so they'll feel like pussies, then you stick in your finger and push out the guts."

"That plastic thing and white stuff?"

"Right. Cut them in rings. Make a basic marinara out of fresh tomatoes, basil, garlic, thyme, red pepper."

"Nothing fresh up here in June, Ralph."

"I don't care. Why don't you send Diana out?"

"Shut up, Ralph. We've been through this before."

"Sticking to your chintzy jealousy, huh? You'll suffocate the poor girl."

"Saw something you'd like for your work. It's called the Jaws of Life. . . ."

"You're late, bub. Already commissioned. I'm using a replica to pull three stuffed penguins out of a burning Pinto. It's a one time thing for an art celebration at Shea Stadium. Should I send tickets?"

7

The dinner had gone rather brilliantly, though Diana had quipped that squid were nature's rubber bands. But she had cleaned her plate! That was the important thing, even if she hadn't returned for seconds or thirds, the cook's ultimate compliment.

Now from the kitchen he could hear her merry laugh, and the laughter of her two close friends, Gretchen and Louise. Frankly, he was in a bit of a huff. It was well past midnight and the girls were eating popcorn and watching Tom Snyder's eagerly awaited discussion with Nancy Friday on the subject of masturbation. Not so long ago, he thought, you'd be horsewhipped talking about your privates on television. "What was the world coming to?" he had asked the girls when they arrived. He was roundly teased for not being in the swing of things. Gretchen weighed two hundred and Louise one hundred. Maybe they did it to each other, for all he knew. He had let his anger run away with him, particularly with that spindly shrike Louise. What a delight it would be to parachute her into darkest Africa where a thousand jigaboos would throw her the pork.

"Admit it, Johnny, you jack off?" she had queried.

"That's none of your business."

"Of course it's my business when you belittle our plans."

"No, I don't. It's adolescent."

"Bullshit. Diana, admit you've caught him at it?"

"Not really."

"Sure, he's too sneaky to be caught. And he's got a sneaky little pile of dirty magazines. . . ."

"Bet you a grand I don't."

"Johnny, you do too." Diana said.

"Both of you put your money where your mouth is."

Diana went to the bedroom to check while Gretchen filtered through the magazine bucket. Louise tapped her foot, breathing hard and righteously through fleering nostrils. Warlock noted that her trousers were pulled up so tightly they revealed her strangely ample labia majora. She flashed a crooked, feral smile as Diana returned with a puzzled look.

"They're gone. And so is the vibrator."

"Touché," he said moving to the kitchen. "I've got some work to bone up on."

"I know he does it. They all do. They unconsciously tweak at their weenies when they read the paper or drive a car. I had Fred do it in front of me to get a little oxygen into our sex life," Louise continued in a snit.

"Johnny, could you make some popcorn?" Gretchen called.

By the time he served the popcorn the girls were in a good mood. Tom had finished talking to Earl Weaver, switched gears, and was full steam with Nancy on masturbation. Louise caught him blushing as he handed her a double-buttered bowl.

"He's blushing," she howled.

"Listen!" Diana and Gretchen were hanging on Nancy's words.

"I leave you charming clam floggers to your program," he said, but they weren't listening.

At the kitchen table Warlock continued to stare into his briefcase while eating a small bowl of popcorn. There was only an empty Chablis bottle, a four day old *Detroit Free Press,* and David Halberstam's book about power. You can't knock power, Warlock thought. He had obviously turned the corner with Hudley through the prudent use of power. The contents of his briefcase, however, didn't reveal a man of power. Those three insouciant girls swam out of the surf and into his brain. Think of them, say . . . in a bathhouse, or in the loft of a cottage, or in a large California-style bathroom. They are beginning to peel off their wet suits when Warlock enters, quite by mistake. No, stay, they say in unison. Dry our backs! They gently strip him and they all hop into the shower. (All his fantasies included a shower to avoid the natural but rather gamy exudate of bodies.) Half the bathroom was carpeted. They said one-potato or eenie-meenie-mynie-moe to see who would go first. Warlock lay down and hoisted one onto his chops while the other slammed down on his rude rouser. There was a knock. No there wasn't. These gratuitous interruptions the mind throws up. He dandled the third with a spare hand. A chorus of moans. He humped all three until they couldn't walk, talk, crawl. Each had exactly seventy-seven orgasms, his lucky number. There was an award banquet.

The program was over and he heard them approach the kitchen chattering. He wedged his hard dick-head under his belt and closed the briefcase with a snap.

"You didn't really miss anything," Louise said. "They pulled their punches."

"Great popcorn." Gretchen quickly finished Warlock's bowl.

Diana scratched his head and he hugged her with energy. His soul was still on the bathroom floor on a nest of three green bathing suits. He stood and gave Louise a firm embrace, making sure she caught the full effect of his rigid wang against her waist. Her eyes widened but for a change she said nothing.

Gretchen and Louise left then, and Warlock led the fair Diana into the living room. He turned out the lights but left on the subtle glare of the TV test pattern. He drew down Diana's jeans and bent her over the leather footrest and whammed away. Then he chewed at her vigorously for a half hour until she kicked over a lamp that had been an obtuse wedding present from his dad. Then they went at it again. It was four A.M. by the time they dragged off to bed.

"See. Wasn't that a lot better than jerking off?"

"They're not mutually exclusive," said Diana, peering into the closet.

"Give me a break."

"Where did you put your magazines?"

"I burned them."

"The diplomas are gone."

"I burned them. And that sex toy, too."

"Are you flipping or something?"

"Just changing my life. I don't want to talk about it until it jells."

"Okay. I love you, darling. It was great."

"But you won't admit it's better?"

"Why does it have to be better? It's just a different thing."

* * *

He awoke from a nightmare at dawn when a thousand song-birds were singing. He felt strong and fearless, having lived through the nightmare and the successful day it had followed. He felt curious and juicy about life which he would continue to meet full tilt and head on. It was warm and Diana was above the sheets, her bare fanny aimed at him like some impossible aperture. If that's not beautiful, what is? he thought.

8

Who was this man? Or who is this man? As he is still very much alive and doing quite well. His wife Diana is also doing very well though she has an uncomfortably close call with death by gunshot wound in the confines of our story. Who could pull the trigger on this gracious beauty? She is five eight, a rare strawberry blonde with green eyes, with Guernsey cream skin, a trifle too much of an overbite to be a fashion model, of Scandinavian-German parentage, fashionably slight breasted, not at all like those pancreatic floozies who grace the smut magazines. Those few who have seen her bending over nude to fetch her clothes are likely to remember it on their deathbed in their respective retirement colonies in Florida, Arizona, California. She possessed a highly strung bottom, and long flawless legs that were extremely strong from managing a succession of unruly riding horses in her youth, and a stint at competitive swimming in high school. Modesty prevents us from discussing her vulva, or perineum—that miniature byway on which either direction is correct.

But she owned a fatal flaw to any man who might come to

know her: from early childhood on she was of a pragmatic bent, passionately wanting to know how things, especially organisms, worked. She helped her father aid in the delivery of calves on his dairy farm. She cleaned chickens, making childish notes on the progress of eggs, from fetid pebbles through tiny marbles, to half inch pearls, finally to the nearly completed egg waiting to be expelled after the chicken lost its head for Sunday dinner. Had her mother not prevented her, she would have autopsied her dead pet dog.

That's not all that bad. Woman's thirst for knowledge. She was the best surgical nurse in northern Michigan and would have become a doctor had she not fallen in love with our hero while a senior in college. She dressed against her beauty when out of uniform, wearing loose fitting sporting clothes and no makeup. She was an ardent supporter of ERA and led a group of like minded women. She despised her vague similarity in looks to Farrah Fawcett and met with anger any fool who commented on it, from humble pump jockeys, to grocers, other nurses, doctors who should have known better. She was bright and graceful to a fault, but her pragmatism frightened her husband who was a Keatsian romanticist. She knew the ways of men and felt it only fair to exercise her own impulses as long as she obeyed the niceties of discretion. Thus at a convention of surgical nurses at the Renaissance Center she bedded a guest speaker in his suite far above the Motor City, in whose streets dope wars raged that would have appalled Billy the Kid, Wyatt Earp, Fu Manchu. She pushed this maven from MIT back on his king sized, mirrored vibra bed, solemnly studied his erect penis until he was nervous, let out a long fugal laugh which was her habit before sex, and sat on it. By dawn he was ready to give up his wife, children, a full professorship. She gave him a peck and said don't be silly. This was one little item her husband would never know, and scarcely reflected promiscuity on her part. It was simply that every year or two since she was married she would meet an especially intelligent man. She was that rare woman who fantasized about Linus Pauling.

Her mate, Johnny Lundgren, John Milton Lundgren, aka Johnny, aka Warlock to himself, a *soupçon* of mystery in a heartland so weather-wicked, so banal that in the midst of winter the populace was given to sucking eggs on Saturday night for want of anything else to do. The local Leelanau Peninsula champion, Don Schneck, went through seven dozen one snowy March evening before projectile vomiting set in, much to the amusement of his belching cronies. Eighty-four raw eggs is quite a whoop.

Johnny was a valedictorian. He owned three guns: a .38 pistol, a .35 Remington deer rifle, a 20-gauge shotgun, all gifts from his father and none of them fired in the past decade. He cleaned and oiled them every Fourth of July when firecrackers reminded him of his neglected weaponry. Johnny owned a large head, large hands and feet, large shoulders and thighs, giving the impression that he was larger than he was. His nose, teeth, and eyes were also outsized. He was a goofy fop and terribly intelligent, no longer to any particular effect.

Of course when you go from forty grand to unemployment you see the elevator continuing to descend far below you. The only thing you lack is the rope around your neck. But they were both desperate to escape Lansing. Excluding the Upper Peninsula, you might regard Michigan as a mitten; anything south of the beginning of the invisible fingers constitutes the industrial and farming flatlands, basically a wretched area resembling the Midlands in England, combining the charmless agribusiness—vast single crop farms—of Ohio and Iowa with factory cities as dim and blighted in their own way as Calcutta: Flint, Lansing, Detroit, Battle Creek, Kalamazoo famed in story and song, Muskegon. Of course these cities are prosperous with labor exacting munificent wages and management living on grandiose sums, but in terms of quality of life it is something like owning the very best, most expensive diving equipment and only having a cesspool or mud puddle to swim in. So they fled to an area that held for Warlock the summer memories of his youth until college: the northland with its crystalline lakes and streams, small villages pervaded by the scent of pine forests that surrounded them, hills, dales, valleys with small marginal farms owned by people not at all unlike their southern counterparts; that is, basically small minded and stupid but possessing a specific archaic attractiveness—nostalgia in the flesh. The catch was, he thought, looking out the window at the small lovely valley, the catch was that the north was growing daily more and more unlike the north of his dream-bound youth. The small farms were steadily being bought up by doctors and stockbrokers for vacation and retirement homes. The quiet lakes were crowded with cottages, and the small villages had begun to affect a false front, mansard-roofed, Swiss chalet look. Solvent hippies had moved in with their arts and crafts boutiques and health food stores—leather and hokum Indian jewelry, groats and granola and magnum vitamins to counteract their drug ingestion. There were even a few shabby communes supported mostly by collective allowances. Back road properties now abounded with No Trespassing signs to protect the swamps and pine barrens from nonexistent intruders, and garish Day-Glo Keep Off signs for nighttime wanderers.

Of course it was all still beautiful compared to anyplace else, or so he consoled himself for the area's inability to cooperate with his dream. Diana loved it without reserve, but then nostalgia was an emotion foreign to her. As an amateur botanist, birdwatcher, butterfly catcher, she knew a great deal more about the natural world than Warlock, who was given always to the large view, and tended to walk around the woods suffused in a trance, remembering where or when he had walked or fished or hunted before. On a mostly subconscious level he was vitally concerned with the world conforming to his idea of it. Once he had decided on something so tentative and idiotic as the evening weather report he was thrown out of step the next day when the report proved inaccurate.

As far as religion was concerned the whole question of God was still up in the air. His father was an atheist of sorts, though he did admit to praying during a typhoon in the South Pacific when he was a radio man on a hospital ship. It was the wounded that made him pray, not his own safety, he insisted. The floating and pitching wounded, the wards awash with vomit, blood, the Pacific. So his father had tried to still the ocean with prayer and the punch line to his story was that it didn't work. In contrast his mother, in the hideous pain of her deathbed, would sing a hymn in Swedish in a high almost querulous voice, then add Glory be to the Father, and to the Son, and to the Holy Ghost:

> Tryggare kan ingen vara
> Än Guds lilla barna
> skara Stjärnanej på himla fästet
> Fågel ej i kändá nästet

Who was this Holy Ghost, Warlock had thought holding her hand as she flopped almost fishlike in terminal pain. It was hard to think of the triumvirate as being particularly friendly when his mother ended life as a flopping fish. His brain was a cloud of ill-formed prayer then and his eyes turned upward to the ceiling and hopefully the sky beyond that, where just as hopefully God and the other two sat or stood and he uttered a prayer for his mother. He didn't have words. It was a capsulated longing for a pre-Adamic earth where mothers could float heavenward in bliss accompanied by flute music and seventy-seven doves.

But he refused to view life as a sequence of setbacks from which no one recovers, save by being safely hidden under six feet of dirt. No. He believed his mother *was* in heaven. If she wasn't, then nothing made any particular sense. He didn't want to be a garden variety cynic. On their last trip to New York he had taken Diana to a revival of *Man of La Mancha.* He was disappointed when she viewed the play as loathsome —in contrast he had tingled with a gentle warmth. There was something to the old saw about grasping for straws.

9

Who is left when everyone is gone? He watched Diana's yellow Volvo disappear toward Traverse City, the faulty muffler putting along after the car disappeared, somehow as lonely as a dog barking far away in the night. Who is left but me standing on the porch on a June morning, and able to see a green leaf fall, for the first and last time, fifty yards away. Am I here if I abolish the input of my five senses? Sure. There's still two hundred pounds of standing meat ignorant of the leaf. The sense of compactness alternated with the banality of worrying about one leaf out of trillions. He had felt a similar sorrow when an area of forest had been flooded long enough to kill the trees —as a child he had talked to trees until a neighbor kid had caught him and told everyone. Water had always been a question of too little, enough, too much. His thought processes lamely trailed off, then returned to the porch. At what point did changing his future merge with eternity itself? Death?

Rather than frighten himself he returned to the safety of the kitchen and a much needed grocery list and a large glass of cheapish but adequate Burgundy. Bread. Potatoes. Death. Orange juice. Eternity. Ivory liquid. Dreams. Garlic, with tarragon wafting into the future. He stopped short of imagining his funeral. He was unaware of the gravity, the unutterable danger of his situation, plucking himself, as he had, out of the manswarm. Heraclitus said that the waking share one common world (cosmos), whereas the sleeping turn aside each man into a world of his own. If a Greek chorus had been present they would have been chanting, in effect: "Woe, a dream is not a map or manual, stupid. Woe, run to the church or psychiatrist. Head for the bar and your favorite beverage, kneel before womankind. Do not separate yourself. Join the army, get a job, help others. Do not act upon this dark secret. Woe, etc."

At the IGA a shadow seemed to pass over him, despite the usual badinage with the wonderful bulbous-nosed butcher who always posed the same resonant question.

"How they hanging, Johnny."

"Buono. Loose. Got this notion there's something right around the corner."

"I was young once. I can't chase pussy with gout. No man can fuck when his foot hurts that bad. It's a known fact."

"Not even for Ava Gardner?"

Warlock mentioned the butcher's favorite, along with Angie Dickinson of *Police Woman.* It was amazing how often Angie came up in northern Michigan. Despite all the youth propaganda it was a forty-seven year old mother who loomed larger than any playmate in minds and peckers of American manhood.

"Johnny, Ava might turn me around but it's doubtful she'll show up here. The fun's over for old Frank." The butcher's face turned so bleak that Warlock felt a melancholy empathy. Then the young, pretty wife of a stockbroker pushed her cart up beside him. She was damp with sweat and wearing a yellow tennis outfit, with little cotton tassles on her shoes. They stared at her so blankly she became flustered and blushed. Warlock grabbed a package of turkey legs.

"You're pretty," he said, not waiting for a reply.

Back home in the kitchen he interrupted a fantasy about the woman in the yellow dress to pour a glass of wine and ponder the problem of turkey legs. He drank deeply What the fuck am I going to do with turkey legs? He had looked at her brown, damp legs and grabbed a package of turkey legs. Perhaps a nourishing soup. Something simple that would calm Diana after a long bloody day of passing weapons to stud butchers. What would she look like in the back of his Subaru in that yellow outfit without undies? Please, Johnny, I need you, she said pointing a Converse skyward. Hot soup it would be.

Unfortunately he fell asleep and the soup boiled down into what luckily bore a resemblance to gravy. He rubbed the sleep from his face and made a cup of coffee. What could he do with a quart of gravy? Why was he sleeping twelve hours out of twenty-four? Shit. He stared at a largish rutabaga Clete had given him from his well stocked root cellar. He felt a sudden surge of creativity.

An hour later he had the rutabaga hollowed out and peeled, albeit clumsily, and filled with gravy as one might fill a Halloween pumpkin without eyes, nose and mouth. He put the rutabaga in the oven with a warm sense of inventiveness, then showered and shaved with further thoughts of the yellow dress, his wang pointing upwards as he shaved. The upright wang and the gravy secreted in the rutabaga gave him a surge of life. It wasn't over yet, by god. He owned the future whose face could be made by the touch of his fingertips. He dressed in a special fuchsia linen shirt, white flannel trousers and Mexican sandals. He made a small pitcher of Margaritas, Diana's favorite, and reread the paper waiting for her return. Something had to be done for these Haitians and Cubans, he mulled.

"Jesus, I'm beat. We had two emergency appendectomies. One had a touch of peritonitis. What a stink."

"Are they going to make it?" His voice was raspy with distaste.

"Probably. Or I hope so. You've got to watch your weight, Johnny. Fat is a big problem on the table."

"I've got the situation in hand, if you don't mind."

"I hope so. Try just eating when you're hungry, rather than out of habit."

"Is that some more of your slant propaganda? You forget who won the war."

"Oh for god's sake. I promise never to mention it again." She crossed the living room and kissed him, her face aglow with the Margaritas. "What smells good? I'm starved. Is it ready?"

He pushed her off his lap and raced to the kitchen. He poked some sprigs of parsley into the softened rutabaga and hauled it to the dining room with a bottle of cold Chardonnay.

"What is it?" she asked sitting down.

"A rutabaga."

"My god!"

"That's not all."

"All?"

"It's full of something." His face glistened with triumph.

"More rutabaga?"

"This is not a joke. Guess."

"A rutabaga heart?"

"Try to get away from your job."

"Oh for god's sake."

"What's my favorite?"

"You have so many. . . ."

"My favorite of favorites. I even have it on toast after Thanksgiving."

"Turkey gravy! But where is it?"

"Voilà!" He slammed down a carving knife, and the dark vault of gravy released itself, perhaps overburdened by sage.

"Smells like our trip to Wyoming. You know, all that purple sage."

"Please taste it, and say something nice."

"Yummy-yummy."

"Diana, goddammit. I said nice."

"Let's make love after dinner. I'm high. No one died today."

10

One morning at breakfast he decided he did not like the notion that he was stewing in his own juices. How can the self measure the self? his ethics professor had questioned so many years back. What a turmoil his mind had been in those years, say from fifteen to twenty-two, and when he had tried to share this turmoil with parents and friends they had failed him with banal accusations such as "you think you're smart." After all, the most obnoxious young people are those who read Thomas Wolfe and take that great burly oaf to heart. In the following generation Kahlil Gibran and Hermann Hesse were to cause fewer problems, albeit their brand of pap seemed to cause early senescence among the young. He had noted this tendency at a convention of wood stove dealers, yet another of his hesitant forays into individual capitalism in the past year.

The convention had started with a "kickoff" breakfast that had included a minister's long-winded prayer about "alternative energy sources" as their scrambled eggs congealed and the coffee cooled. The minister signed off with a hearty "keep the home fires burning" and everyone fell to their breakfasts as

Eskimo dogs do, rumor has it, to a fresh human turd. Then they all sang "Hi Neighbor" and made their way to separate seminars in such subjects as "Chimney Safety," "Making Use of Lowly Conifer," "Whither the Future of Wood Burning," "The New Market of the Poor." It seems that wood-burning stoves were a middle-class phenomenon and the poor couldn't be persuaded to ante up a half grand at minimum for fifty bucks worth of cast iron, no matter the obvious economic benefits. Wood was absurdly cheap in northern Michigan and out-of-state delegates from Vermont, New Hampshire, New York, were in a jealous snit about it. Lundgren-Warlock publicly questioned the difference between twenty-five a face cord for split hardwood in Michigan and a hundred and twenty-five in the East. He was attacked roundly by an eastern contingent of woodchoppers who all seemed to own master's degrees in creative writing for some reason. They took umbrage at his question, as if they were price gouging, which is exactly what he had in mind. Then he tried to withdraw with the witticism that there seemed, at any event, to be a nigger in the woodpile. This brought shrieks of racism, and even sexism, from a burly chainsaw freak of the feminine sex. Lundgren reddened, and pondered a strategic withdrawal. He wandered down the hall into a seminar called "The Philosophy of Woodburning." The conversation there tended toward the more austere aspects of ecology; the American Indians who unfortunately were becoming "old" in the manner of the Budweiser Clydesdales, the sacred fires that burned ceaselessly through human history. It reminded him somewhat of the gay movement building a philosophical system out of their wee-wees. He remembered helping his grandfather who would go out to the back forty to cut wood to keep the house warm because it was cold outside.

But the self could measure the self under the most rigid circumstances, he thought. Life drew certain lines, it wasn't some big glob of mashed potatoes. His clear view of change, of the perimeters of the future, owned a strong enough religious impulse to lead him inevitably to rule making. He took a law tablet and ballpoint pen from the briefcase.

Number One. EAT SPARINGLY

He thrummed the growing ring of lard around his waist. Writing this first rule made him feel thinner. Eating crept up on him and had become his major source of pleasure outside of, perhaps, making love to Diana. To men in prison food is the central morale factor. Bad food causes riot and death. In El Paso weekend passes in the Air Force had sent men braying the restaurants, thence to bars, thence to the whorehouses of Juarez, thence to all night Mexican restaurants for more food. Then there was a tendency to vomit and fall asleep wherever one was. Lundgren was always the driver in that he never vomited. But then the Air Force had ended his art career and had only been to his father an acceptable hedge before he entered the real world. Eat Sparingly because he felt gluttony was creeping up from all flanks. On the far side of the table were the remains of a laboriously made Louisiana chicken hash. Too much Tabasco had necessitated a beer. Two beers, in fact. He must now fight the urge to nap, fight any plans for an unnecessary lunch, though the pig hocks he'd poached the night before nestled sweetly in their own juices in the refrigerator. NO! And there was another darker thought: maybe he was running out of hormones. He had read about something called testosterone in *Playboy* but it reminded him of tsetse flies, the bane of the tropics. He remembered getting a mosquito bite on his dick at boy scout camp. Diana would be home late from work and had requested something simple. Poach a chicken with noodles maybe. Stuff a sirloin with oysters and broil it. Not simple. Hot and crispy Hunanese fish? Nope. *Grabure*, an ascetic vegetable soup with braised oxtails? Probably.

Number Two. AVOID ADULTERY

Flagging appetites always summon up the iridescent vision of variety. Someone else. There was a certain smallish cheerleader type who worked at the Unemployment Office who had mentioned that she bowled at Timberlanes on Thursday nights. Her face was pointed and her butt bobbed. Pistons. No, he thought, I got more than I can handle at home, a saw not less true for being so often repeated. Adultery was messy, both in the inevitably sneaky structure of carrying it off and in the emotional messiness that followed. He'd best keep his nose to the grindstone of the future. What about the grindstone of Patty, the Unemployment Office cheerleader and champ bowler? Probably a pretty grindstone. It was a bold man that ate the first oyster, his dad used to quote from Swift. An Apalachicola oyster. A Bélon. A Bon Secour. An ordinary Chesapeake. Today was Thursday. Make the soup and leave a note saying you're having a drink with Cletis. Clete would cover. Sure he was with me, not that Diana would check. Call Patty and arrange arrival at lanes at last minute so as not to loiter with the dummies. Then to a tourist cabin where he would roger her little joints loose. His dick rose with his despair. It seemed the act of making a coda defiled the spirit of the coda.

Number Three. DO YOUR BEST IN EVERYTHING

This was easy, since he was doing nothing. But wasn't readjusting the future a man's work? Of course. It required infinite wit and intelligence. And the little things. His mother said do little things well like mowing lawns and washing cars and then you'll be ready for the big things. Like marriage and job. He warmed to the idea that he was good at marriage and had been good at his job. And he was fast becoming quite the cook. Everything was all systems go for this great voyage into the future. The future or bust.

Number Four. GET IN FIRST RATE SHAPE

The chicken hash sat heavy in his gut. Jogging was corny. Perhaps long hikes in the outback alone with his dog. And gun. And compass. No snacks. Maybe a canteen of water. He took the *Free Press* to the bedroom and lay back with a dark sigh. Buy a set of weights. Do yoga exercises with Diana. Fuck her in one of those weird positions. Why had he thrown away his dirty magazines? Walk ten miles a day and learn the ways of nature. Row a boat all the way around Lake Leelanau. Thirty miles. Hudley would like the boat. Go from two hundred to one seventy-seven, an harmonious figure. Meet Patty in the woods. Eat yogurt. Eat raw deer meat. Eat cottage cheese. Snore.

11

"You show all the symptoms of a classic depression."

Diana dropped this verbal shitbomb right in the middle of the oxtail-vegetable soup. He used perhaps a teaspoon of freshly grated horseradish in each of his bowls. She had caught him staring slackjawed at the ceiling with his spoon suspended over the bowl. His eyes dropped to hers, viewing her almost as an attractive stranger.

"Did I hear you correctly?"

"I don't know. What did I say?"

"That your father was buying classic cars as a hedge against inflation."

"I said you were showing all the signs of a classic depression."

"You said symptoms. I heard you the first time."

"It's no laughing matter, Johnny. I think you need professional help."

"A whore? A psychiatrist?"

"I talked to a doctor friend to confirm my suspicions. He agreed."

"You talked to some fucking sawboner about me? How dare you."

"I needed to talk to somebody. I took the liberty of making an appointment for you on Friday."

"Not a chance. Cancel it. Is this doctor buddy someone you're screwing at lunch hours?"

"Very paranoid and not very funny. You've been dawdling for months. You're not happy up here and maybe we should move back downstate where there are more opportunities. . . ."

"Not a fucking chance. They're not driving me out of here."

"No one's trying to drive you anywhere. You go to the grocery store and cook dinner. That's it."

"You don't like your dinners?"

"That's not what I mean. You're defensive."

"Not an odd move under attack. I suggest you stick to twirling guts and avoid cheap psychologizing. Remember your specialty is the body not the mind. You know how cows think, not humans."

The veiled reference to her farm background sent a full bowl of soup into his face. She stomped toward him and hissed into his face.

"You stupid fucking jerk."

Some of the soup drizzled down his neck to his tummy. He dammed it there with a palm while wiping barley, celery, tomato, a shred of meat from his face. He heard Diana race up the stairs to her secret room. The door locked with a clack. He went to the bathroom in a daze, washed up, changed his shirt and combed his hair. What to do next? He put on his overcoat and walked up the stairs. Utterly without intention, he delivered a karate kick with all his weight, exploding the secret door off its hinges. There was a scream. He didn't look in.

On the way to the bowling alley a single tear fell. He stopped at Dick's Pour House for two quick doubles. His heart was thumping unnaturally and he reflected that his life insurance was up to date. Two hundred grand worth. Diana would be happier without him. She would probably marry a doctor.

At the bowling alley parking lot he paused for a moment, then moved quickly inside like an assassin. He gave Patty a dark look and she followed him outside in her pleated skirt, bowling shoes, and a shirt that not oddly had PATTY emblazoned across the back. She jumped in the car beside him and they fell into each other's arms.

"Let's go to a motel."

"I can't. I got one more game. I can't let the girls down."

He started the car but she grabbed the keys and the car died with a grinding ignition squawk. She smelled of pee, talc, sweat and beer. She turned on the overhead light and stared at him down her pert, pointed snout, her head held high.

"Nobody pushes me, Johnny."

He replied by pushing a paw up under her skirt and working two fingers in around her panties. She crooned and swiveled, burying the fingers to the hilt. He added a third as an afterthought. She leaned forward and delivered a not altogether pleasant French kiss. She backed away with misty eyes and flicked off the overhead light.

"You smell like vegetable soup."

"Vegetable-oxtail soup. My wife threw a bowl of it in my face."

"Poor Johnny. I hope you kicked her in the cunt." She deftly unzipped his fly, unleashing his limp noodle. "Let me give you a quick B.J. to get the pressure off. Then wait in the bar. I got that one more game and then we can go to a motel and go all the way."

As she fell to, Warlock reflected on woman's inhumanity to woman. He had never struck a woman and couldn't imagine kicking the fair Diana in the cunt. In fact, he longed for her and tried to imagine that Patty's furious mouth was Diana's, but Patty was far more experienced, having perfected the rare technique of deep throat. Unfortunately there was a deep, glottal coughing sound to her technique and his imagination went far afield in order to come off: he was thirteen and at their summer cottage, the last time he played Indian doctor with the pretty thirteen year old a few cabins down. They were in a cave of logs, and on a bed of ferns with the sun dappling down through the poplar and oak. She was Marsh Hawk and he was Warlock. He drew down her shorts while she was anesthetized under secret herbs and he chewed at her sparse furze for the first time. Amazingly, she writhed around and he said you're supposed to be out cold. She returned the favor and he permanently lost his soul to women with one long screech that shot through the forest, echoing in gulleys and across the lake like that of his namesake, the Warlock. When he opened his eyes to take her into his arms she was gone.

When he opened his eyes after the door snap he watched Patty trot across the parking lot and into the bowling alley. He drove toward home with an inexpressibly heavy heart, stopping again at Dick's for two double shots. The bartender asked him with an air of ennui what he thought about the Tigers' chances. "Nil," he said cryptically. "They never should have traded George Kell."

* * *

Diana sat on the couch with red eyes in a mauve, flower-printed bathrobe. She was reading Corbin's classic on Sufism in Avicenna. She was not given to magazines and light reading. He knelt down and she wordlessly caressed his head. She smelled like violets and creeks in May. He kissed her knee and thought, this is Diana's knee—she is not me, nor I her.

"I've been a fool. I'm sorry."

"I love you, Johnny. I was trying to help."

"I'll fix your door."

"What door?"

He felt a rippling of nausea, distinctly remembering kicking down her door. His foot still hurt.

"I know it. I was just teasing," she laughed. "Do me with all your clothes on." She took off her robe and nightgown.

He worked away, sweating jubilantly in his wool shirt and overcoat, staring into her closed eyes. Something new.

12

He dressed quickly in a lightweight vicuña shirt, cavalry twill trousers, cordovon brogans, an English cut suede jacket—all, he felt, subtly understated and appropriate for the Unemployment Office, then on to the Jaws of Life barbecue where he would meet Diana who was one of the hostesses for the fundraising event. With effort he waved away a stroke of tedium. Life in the great north wasn't all beer and skittles and appearances were important.

Not to indicate that he was simpleminded: his "negative" selling point centered in his weaving and dipping, his nonconcentric explosions. Contrary to his dialogue with Diana which would lead one to slap his face for stupidity, Lundgren-Warlock could talk like the late Adlai Stevenson when called upon to do so. Diana preferred him to be down to earth and he teased her with commonplace idiocies, as frequently bored, childless couples will play word games.

Only the month before in early May he had demonstrated this potential opaqueness in a job interview at an automobile dealership. The unemployment agency files had clearly advertised a managerial position which turned out to be another salesman's job. The owner was a large, florid Irishman out of Notre Dame as so many auto dealers in the Midwest are, clearly showing the effects of four decades of alcohol and perhaps a missing gene or two. The dealer noted Lundgren-Warlock's understated J. Press suit and Paul Stuart shirt and thought he might have snared a class, WASP item, someone who would be a capable glad-hander to the local professional class. The dealer offered a cup of instant coffee into which Lundgren-Warlock dumped a plastic teaspoonful of Pream. In short, they didn't hit it off through no one's fault.

"What are your general aims, past or present?"

"Aims? A generally mechanistic term, don't you think?"

"Not sure I know what you mean."

"Mean? I mean something like the meaning of meaning." Lundgren-Warlock relaxed in his chair. He didn't want to sell automobiles and had a spare hour before lunching with Diana at the hospital cafeteria. "When I hear the word aim I think of aiming a shotgun at a grouse, the three-by-nine Bushnell variable scope on my .35 at a deer."

"You like to hunt?" The dealer hoped to get the man back to earth. Maybe he hunted, hence was putatively normal.

"Yes and no," he continued. "Aim also reminds one of B-29 bombsights. Or Von Neumann's solution to the tracking gun which did as much as nuclear fission to end World War Two."

"I was thinking more of your ambitions?"

"To bring home the bacon, pure and simple. Pure venality. But then I think of the fatalism of Keynes and Samuelson, how at my retirement age in twenty-three years it will take an estimated fifty thousand a year to put a youngster through a year of college." He loved to invent statistics, his favorite being that every year in the United States more people die of bad mayonnaise than rattlesnake bite. There was the rare Oklahoma case where a man became violently ill from suppurating potato salad, fell retching in the weeds, and was bitten by a record-sized Eastern diamondback.

"We sell a good product. Anything is possible. By then the commission on a vehicle might be five grand. You won't have any trouble sending the kids to college."

"But the youngest of my two will be thirty-eight in 2000. I presume she'll be finished with college by then. In reality I actually don't have children."

Now the dealer was lost in his thoughts. He felt put upon. It seemed to be raining in his heart. He thought about his trip to Ireland the summer before. One dawn while his wife slept, he left the hotel and accompanied an old man on his horse-drawn milk run. He had felt wonderful lifting the cans of fresh milk onto the wagon.

"Get out of here, you crazy fucker," the dealer had said in an Irish brogue that came out of the walls.

"Just remember, Subaru is going to leave you guys eating shit for years to come," Lundgren had replied—simply "Lundgren" at the time because it was another month before he would regain Warlock by virtue of a dream.

As he stood at his Subaru door in the yard of their rented farmhouse certain doubts arose. How did one maintain the purity of vision, say as an anchorite gives himself to Christ forever and forever, let alone the almost science fiction job of changing your own future? He looked up at the spreading maples and noted how quickly the pastels of May enriched themselves into the deep greens of June. The alfalfa field next to the driveway was a din of bees. Staring at the impenetrable shield of leaves above him he thought how in the movies of his youth the crown of a sorry battle-torn coconut tree could hide a Jap sniper. Battle weary Sgt. Luke Fisk of Lawrence, Kansas, would amble by the tree and get his brains blown out despite his cumbersome helmet. Warlock's father had told him that Japs could hide in these trees because their heads looked like coconuts. Any fool knew that. After the movie they always had a chocolate soda at Bonsal's drugstore.

It would take some concentration he thought, sliding into the car. The human mind is not easy to push around. For instance, standing in the yard and thinking about how to change the future his brain had lost itself in maple leaves, then on to World War II and coconuts. He still didn't like coconut in any form. Diana did a certain form of Oriental meditation up in her attic hideout, her private place. Her old college friend, Gretchen, had started her on it, along with a preoccupation with some truly nasty health foods. The door to the attic was, not incidentally, kept locked. The first time in their seven year marriage that she had slapped his face was when he had quite drunkenly teased her about keeping a "date with a dildo" in her room.

Jesus Christ! He slammed his hand against the dashboard. Keep to the future! His anger cracked reality and allowed a little mystery of the night and dawn to enter again. He stared hard beyond the insect splats on the windshield. Indians, he remembered. Sometimes warriors would do everything backwards when they went stale. But he could scarcely drive the twenty miles to Traverse City in reverse, and in forward there weren't any new routes he hadn't taken before. He had to change the nature of his mind first, then other changes would occur. This was a minor stroke of lightning, equal to touching an electric fence, unwarily, at night.

He slammed the Subaru into four-wheel drive and moved it deliberately across the lawn where the aerial whipped against the clothesline. He skirted most of the alfalfa field, circled through the orchard, and put the little station wagon through its paces, crossing a creek and a ditch and up onto the road, throwing two streams of dirt the last ten yards. He felt a certain sense of victory.

13

Then life changed with as little reason as it had previously refused to change. He got up very early in the morning after the Jaws of Life barbecue, and drove south with Hudley forty-five miles to Kingsley. He was equally shattered by his behavior and a hangover so severe that he rated it in the top five of his life. The single grace note was the remnant of a dream, some shred of vision about being unable to pull a plow because there were three glass slides between vertebrae up and down his spine. In his dream he was able to pull out the obstructions and felt a vast surge of power in his sleep.

After the first few miles the dog began barking at passing cars. Hudley owned a resonant, basso bark that made Warlock clench his jaws until they hurt. At a traffic light in Traverse City he grabbed the dog by the scruff of the neck and shook him vigorously.

"Give me a break, Hud. I got a top fiver."

The dog fell silent, then licked Warlock's cheek in sympathy. Warlock had always been interested in ratings; in his youth he had charted on graph paper all the professional sports teams, in addition to the top forty pop tunes. Like model airplane building, kite flying, the soap box derby, it was essentially a dead-end preoccupation. When he grew five inches in his fourteenth year his graph indicated he would be nine foot three by twenty-one, certainly a capable foe for the great Minneapolis center, George Mikan. Perhaps he would live in Chicago, high above the city with the early playmate Janet Pilgrim, who would see the sensitive person behind the towering height. He would be desirable to all women but would probably stay faithful to Janet, except on extended roadtrips when his huge body would no longer be able to control its dark gorilla lust and cheerleaders would line up at his hotel door crooning their cheers for attention.

This morning he felt so battered he somehow knew that he needed the wilderness even though what he thought of as wilderness included a twinge of fright for him. It wasn't actually wilderness but a huge river bottom area that included some hundred thousand acres of abused scrub forest, crisscrossed with log roads. After a long walk he intended to stop and seek the counsel of his old friend, Cletis Griscombe, a unilaterally stable carpenter, bricklayer, hunter and fisherman.

He turned the car off the blacktop onto a bumpy two track, slipping it into four-wheel drive. Hud snorted deeply at the unpeopled air, his ridiculously acute senses ready for any challenge.

"Slow down, big stallion. We're going swimming."

They were passing through a clearing in the forest, a verdant June meadow, when Hudley suddenly flung himself through the open window with a roar. Warlock was sunken in thoughts that Michigan license plates aptly read Winter-Water Wonderland, and it took a moment or two to swerve to a halt and give chase. The dog was a blur heading for a small grassy knoll a hundred yards distant, upon which some small woodland creature was frittering away the morning. Warlock made a good fifty yard burst, screaming "Hud," but the dog was already shaking the creature, finishing it off with a high toss in the air, then grabbing it and trotting in a proud circle. It was a plump female woodchuck with small pink teats peeking through the fur. The woodchuck's eyes were open and Warlock grabbed it by the neck and a tug-of-war ensued with the dog shaking its head so violently that Warlock's shoulder ached. The limp neck in his grasp told Warlock that the poor woodchuck was deader than a doornail. The dog raced off toward the car with his prize.

"Hud, you fuck, it's a girl," he muttered following the dog to the car with glum thoughts about nature being all tooth and claw. He had been a fan of Ralph Waldo Emerson and Albert Schweitzer in college and despised violence of any sort. When he neared the car the dog scooted underneath growling and chewing on his prize. He lit a cigarette and reflected that the evening before he hadn't been a noble enough person to walk away from a fight. He had behaved grotesquely like his dog and his face reddened in the sunny glade at the memory of women screaming.

The untoward event had happened rather early in the evening at the barbecue. He was standing with two flirtatious, middle-aged doctors' wives watching the cooks broil two hundred chickens using margarine, he thought disparagingly, instead of the butter, garlic, tarragon, white wine, lemon, he favored with chicken. There was a large open bar and an assortment of doctors, medical personnel, and businessmen were downing drinks with surprising alacrity to get their money's worth. On a dais behind the bar sat the grand machine itself, the Jaws of Life. Warlock imagined its mighty claws freeing innocent children from crushed vehicles. He warmed to the party and could have charmed the pants off the two women if he had wanted to. But suddenly a raucous voice called out his name. It was the auto dealer who had hosted the unpleasant interview, accompanied by two large oafs in string ties who were, no doubt, salesmen. Warlock turned from the women, the setting sun partially blinding him.

"There's mister fancy-dan jerkoff, boys. We'll starve that jerkoff out. He'll hightail it downstate. We'll keep his wife up here." He finished with a sequence of hearty yuks.

Warlock's brain hummed with rage and he glanced around at the appalled spectators who were murmuring their disapproval of the auto dealer. Warlock quickly reflected that he couldn't hit a man in his sixties. There was a pile of partially thawed chickens waiting their turn on the grill. He carefully selected one and, as a former high school pitcher and American Legion sandlot champ, he hurled a three pound chicken fastball into the auto dealer's face. The throw poleaxed him. The first salesman oaf charged and was felled by a kick, and the second one wandered in lamely, knowing that he was outfaced. Warlock boxed his ears with cupped open hands, his father having taught him that severe ear pain disarms attackers.

The two women led him away, clucking to everyone his exonerating praise. Diana was furious, but was quickly soothed by the fact that even the most intelligent women love winners. He was brought a succession of whiskey to calm his adrenaline and Diana introduced him to the famed inventor, Doctor Rabun.

"I feel vindicated. That fool swindled me in a car deal. Thank you," the good doctor had said.

"It was easy. I was cornered."

Then the music started and a number of ladies wanted to dance with the hero. Warlock in his whiskey haze noted that he could see no panty line under Diana's dress. He felt terribly sexy suddenly, and pondered the chances of slipping her off into the shrubbery for a quicky. Nil. By the time the party ended he felt cheated in the car because he hadn't had his half chicken.

He kneeled on the two track and peered at Hudley's blood-grizzled maw. The dog's eyes flashed and he growled at his master, reverting on a warm June morning to the completely feral.

"I'm giving you five minutes, then we're going to kick ass." He crept around the car to the other side but the dog, too, had deftly changed positions. He couldn't drive off without running over the dog. It was a Mexican standoff and now he wanted something to eat and a cold beer. Clete ate fried woodchuck. No frying pan. No beer. No oil. And the woodchuck was in shreds. He reached in the car and laid on the horn, a noise that normally drove the dog crazy, but he only hurt his own head. He got in the car, started it, and edged forward, his heart beating and mouth dry. He continued creeping ahead, noting the dog continuing to chew in the rearview mirror. When the dog was a speck he got up and raced after the car. Warlock floored it until he reached the river, nearly a mile away. He parked his car in a grove of white birches and undressed. He was halfway down a sandbank when the dog appeared at top speed with the woodchuck still in its mouth. Warlock ignored the dog and descended into the cold clear water, carried along by the swift current to an eddy near the far bank. The dog followed eagerly, his jaws gripping the wet carcass. Warlock firmly held the dog by the neck and dunked him until the woodchuck's body was released and floated downstream. He let go of the dog who nipped his forearm in a survival frenzy. The offended dog swam back across the river and jumped into the car. It was snoring soundly when Warlock dressed and drove off. His own mind was quarreling over what restaurant in Traverse City might offer a few drinks and the least repellent lunch.

14

In the evening he pushed away the *Free Press* and Jack Anderson's abrasive column when only half finished. Criticism wasn't enough, somebody had to take the bull by the horns, as his dad used to say. He read Anderson to keep on his political toes, but now a thousand words of carping about bureaucratic toadies in Washington seemed less than apropos.

After swimming he had stopped at Clete's to say hello, and the vulnerability of his hangover, in addition to all the recent violence, had made him feel weak and strange. He found Clete standing with bow and arrow beside his crystalline spring fed trout pond. The trout were fed on pellets and couldn't be caught on flies and worms because flies and worms didn't smell or look like pellets. Clete would throw pellets to bunch up the trout, then shoot an arrow attached to a string into their midst.

"Want a shot?"

"Nope. No thanks."

"You look like you been boiled in shit."

"Thanks. I'm not at the top of my form."

"What's wrong?"

"I think I'm going to change my life."

"Good idea."

"Why?"

"You're not doing anything. Not hard to improve on a vacuum."

"You got a point. I've got some ideas."

"Every time I pass the cemetery on the way to work I get the feeling we don't live forever."

"You're probably right."

They ate fried trout and some homemade bread and butter washed down with glasses of George Dickel whiskey. Warlock offered up a long keening explanation of his life but stopped when he noted Clete was dozing. In the summer Cletis worked up to sixteen hours a day as a block layer and had a tendency to doze when not immediately engaged. Then he raised one eye with a quip.

"Don't you know everyone's life is shit? You're smart enough to do something about your own. Don't be such a drag-ass."

On the way home it occurred to him he didn't want to be a drag-ass. Advice of any sort had always been particularly difficult for him in that there seemed such a tremendous abyss between the wisdom of advice and reality. In grade school he always confused reality and realty, staring in silent confusion from the back of their two-tone '47 Chevy, as his father drove past a realty office.

And there was a sacred flavor to advice, whether it was the Ten Commandments, the Sermon on the Mount, an officer in the Air Force advising him to scrub his weenie with hydrogen peroxide after a trip to Juarez, his father telling him to abandon art in favor of business because "art didn't dollar up on the hoof," which summoned up a vision of a painting of a field full of fat steers that no one would ever buy. Art was the runt pig in the far corner of the pen; the last to shyly feed on the stray kernels of corn buried in the mud. Art had been cruel when he was finishing his M.B.A. and living with Marilyn, his first wife. They lived in a small, Spartan apartment in a married-student compound and he worked long hours at the desk of the business library to augment the small salary of his teaching assistantship. It was a warm spring evening and he could smell the flowers of the horticultural garden through the window. With the aid of Dexamyl spansules he had finished a long master's thesis on the irrationality of the small-business tax the evening before. For the first time in two years he was left with nothing to do, so he wandered up to Arts and Letters on his cigarette break. An attractive, rather Levantine looking girl in rakish bangs had suggested he read the recently published *Doctor Zhivago*. He preferred something more racy, frankly prurient, but didn't want to admit it to the girl. It was a heartrending three days: the novel virtually overhauled him, pulled his pistons and ground his fatigued valves. He moaned around in disgust with business trying to recapture the nobility of the palette he had ignored for two years. He refused to attend the commencement exercises that featured Richard Nixon as speaker. The onerous responsibilities of being a junior executive in data processing—did not the great Gauguin work at the Bourse?—freed him of his melancholy, though when the movie came out there was a resurgence. It would be a bitch to choose between Geraldine Chaplin and Julie Christie, be a doctor, turn out your art, all during the Revolution, he had thought.

But the most poignant advice had come from the year before

when he had flown to New York with a trustee for a two day meeting. He hadn't liked the idea of the trip because he had thought the trustee to be a weird duck, an electronics inventor who had dealt for years with the Defense Department and owned a small consulting firm which served as a think tank. The trustee turned out to be shrewd and elliptic at the same time, talking in riddles like the guys in Diana's so-called wisdom books in Zen. Though their plane seats were first class, Vergil, the trustee, drew from a rucksack a lunch bucket and a bottle of white wine, a chunk of game paté he had made out of duck and woodcock, some coarse bread, and a small jar of sour French pickles called *cornichons.* He made Warlock compare the airplane fodder to this food. Vergil was slender and wiry, an unlikely gourmet. "You have to eat at least twice a day all your life. I never under any condition settle for swill. Eating well is my magic potion for my morale, brain and pecker." He patted his lap as he explained this to Warlock (Johnny Lundgren then). Vergil interviewed him on his diet and recommended he eschew quantity in favor of quality. They were interrupted for a half hour while the old goat flirted with the stewardesses. When they entered the La Guardia landing pattern Vergil suddenly turned grave.

"I've been watching you for two years, son. At first I thought you had a certain flair, that you were different from these barking nitwits the world calls businessmen." Vergil gestured at the entire contents of the big plane, and it did seem that everyone yipped and barked. He fell silent then, closing his eyes.

"And I'm not?" Warlock asked.

"You might be someday but you need a trial by fire, a momentous event that will shake the loose shit out of your brain. You don't live in the actual world. You live in a far inferior world where you dissipate all your energies making the world conform to your wishes. You spend all your time in yearning, in rehearsals, in forming tepid, unwarranted opinions. I know I'm right. I was like you once. . . ."

"What did you do?" Warlock interrupted.

"You might find out. It's a little different for everyone it happens to."

Vergil reminded him now of Dr. Rabun. They were obviously cut from the same cloth. Rabun was a crank, an eccentric, a doctor who had never practiced but had a wide reputation as an inventor of medical devices: valves and filters for kidney machines, a system for computerized blood testing, storage equipment for glands awaiting transplant, an absurdly effective prosthetic device for men made impotent by severe diabetes and other biological rather than imaginary causes, and several podiatric improvements. There was a trace of irony to Dr. Rabun's severe foot problems. All this Warlock learned at the barbecue dance. Evidently Rabun's appearance was a rare one and doctors who are ordinarily close mouthed to those outside their magic circle of affluence and power spoke to Warlock rather freely. Of course he realized this was due to his connection to the center of attention that evening—Diana, whose soft clinging pale green sheath dress and athletic dancing mannerisms were a show stopper. The middle-aged medics who had seen far too many fat ladies in the stirrups edged toward her all the while trying to maintain some decorum like deferential iron filings to an implacable magnet. Many crafty souls conversed with Warlock as a ploy but they were all beat to the target by a stud proctologist, famed as sort of an AMA Don Juan. And all the dowdy wives muttered, covered with bogus looking jewelry that was actually real. Warlock danced with these pre- and postmenopausal birds, some of surprising though fading loveliness. He liked older women for the simple reason that they were less likely to be dumb. Ripeness is all, he remembered someone saying, the deceptive joy of the windfall apple. From these he learned that Rabun was much disliked by the medical fraternity, despite their obvious toadying on this particular evening. In his rare statements to the press Rabun was outrageous: on a recent occasion the inventor had stated that most doctors were bloodthirsty boobs that should be practicing out of barbershops like they did in the Middle Ages. The last dance of the evening was a shock to everyone. Rabun got up from the chair he had spent the entire evening in, being nasty and drinking endless cups of champagne punch. He cut in on the flashy proctologist and claimed the traditional waltz with Diana. It was rather touching; Rabun's tall, knobby, saturnine figure in a well-cut tuxedo, but in shoes that looked like weirdly inflated Hush Puppies, draped around the regal Diana, painfully but somehow arrogantly out of step, his eyes blind to the audience.

15

He awoke to a flickering test pattern and a dog's bark. He had made popcorn, then sat down to watch *Saturday Night Live*, and had fallen asleep with the large bowl of popcorn on his lap. Now the bowl was empty and he imagined that Hudley had crept up upon him and had finished it off because the usual ample supply of congealed butter had vanished from the bowl's bottom; an easy solution to a puzzle that might present a mystery to someone with less wit. His father had gone from small town police chief to crack detective in Minneapolis. It might somehow be in his own blood to become a great detective. That would certainly be changing his future in a single fell swoop. The steps on the porch had to be Diana's because Hudley was madly wiggling his bottom and dogs recognized steps. Could a man learn to recognize steps? Probably, if he sufficiently attuned his senses, heretofore atrophied by sloth and self-indulgence. There was an electric coolness in his head as Diana burst in the door. She kissed him, per usual.

"I'm sorry I'm so late. I called but no one answered. I hope you weren't worried."

"What time did you call?"

"About an hour and a half ago. I have some exciting . . ."

"I was walking the dog," he interrupted. The fact is the phone never woke him.

"I got some exciting news. Doctor Rabun called this morning at the hospital for your resumé. I drove home at lunch and picked it up, then dropped it off after work."

"Three hours is quite the drop-off."

"I went in for a drink. There was a couple there from France and we talked a long time."

"I'll bet."

"He wants to meet you tomorrow at nine to talk about a job."

"Tomorrow is Sunday," he said blankly. "We usually sleep in and sort of fool around."

"Johnny, why are you being so difficult? This is a rare opportunity."

He got up and flicked the TV dial to tune in the remains of Melvoin's *Creature Feature* on Channel 29, then walked into the kitchen. His mood was still coolish but things were changing so fast that he needed a drink. "What does he need, someone to paint a boat, or wash a car?" he called from the kitchen, affecting Travis McGee's laconic cynicism. Diana walked to the bathroom without looking at him.

"He wants a troubleshooter," she said, slamming the door and turning on the shower.

He sat down, repressing the urge to peek through the keyhole to see her take off her nurse's outfit, a vice he indulged himself in occasionally. You don't need a peek when you got the whole package. There was a flash of a troublesome thought: his former secretary had confessed to him that she knew her husband was cheating when he took a shower the minute he got home to cleanse himself of the evidence. Perhaps the nose was a neglected instrument of intelligence. The bird dog finds the wee woodcock in the thickest of thickets and Hudley senses a bitch in heat over a mile away. Could a man develop super smell? It would be a disadvantage around toilets, unless one could turn it off and on, he conjectured, moderating his idea. Besides, Diana wouldn't select a man in his sixties. Being married to a beautiful woman wasn't all beer and skittles. Frequently at restaurants, parties, department stores, theater lines, he sensed the leer, the lust in men's eyes. He was pleased that her involvement in the women's movement included wearing clothes that deemphasized her sexuality. The exception was that she often neglected to wear undergarments and that upset him. "What if we get in a car accident?" he asked.

"I've seen a lot of accident victims. None of the girls were thinking about panties," she replied.

Yet another version of *Dracula* was concluding on *Creature Feature* as the shower stopped. The whiskey mellowed him and he was aroused. Why did people love Dracula? Warlock never wanted to bite a woman in the neck, and in his entire life had never conjured up a single rape fantasy. When Diana's lib friends were on the muscle about rape he liked to remind them that there hadn't been a single rape on the police files in Leelanau County in the past decade. Gretchen said that there had been an attempted rape five years before, but the guy couldn't get a hardon. Without thinking Warlock had replied "that's his problem" and they had brayed him into retreating into the kitchen to make them snacks. They insisted that most rapes were not reported, and the police files were only the tip of the iceberg. He brought in the Nachos and replied that up here there wasn't a tip to indicate an iceberg and that their arguments were tautological. When they demanded he define "tautological" he discovered he had forgotten—Philosophy 203 was a long time ago. His trump card was to call his father, the great detective, in Minneapolis.

"Dad, what about rape?"

"Did you rape someone, Johnny?"

"No, Dad. I'm in an argument with Diana's friends."

"I'm watching *Monday Night Football*. Johnny, I need to get away from the job."

"Sorry, I just need a few facts. They got me in a corner."

"Jesus, Earl Campbell just blasted the shit out of this linebacker. . . . Okay I see a lot of it. Short of murder and kidnap it's the worst crime. You should see these weeping, screaming girls and women, even old ladies. A lot of them have torn vaginas and anuses and are beaten black and blue. It's not a particularly sexual crime but a result of child abuse, urban blight, loneliness, vengeance. A lot of victims end up in the nuthatch and are never okay again. . . . Jesus, is Bum Phillips pissed. He's out there yelling at the ref."

"Thanks, Dad."

"Is that good enough? To me it's the worst crime. I usually kick the shit out of a hot or confirmed suspect when I'm sure. We had a little girl last week that took fifteen stitches in her butt and lost an eye. You find a job?"

"I'm on the verge, Dad."

"Good luck, son. Turn on the TV and skip the rape shit."

"I love you, Dad."

"I love you, too, son. Keep your pecker up."

He was fair minded enough to hang up the kitchen phone

and try to admit to the group that he was wrong, but by then they were discussing the perils facing the ERA vote.

Now Diana emerged from the bathroom in a short cotton nightie with a towel around her head. She sat down on the couch and started rubbing lotion on her legs, drawing one foot up onto the couch. There was something about heat that made a man lustful. One hot summer night years ago they'd drunk a great deal and she had put on a scanty outfit he had ordered from Los Angeles from a small ad in *Penthouse* magazine. She had added garish makeup and danced in a garter belt. He had worried about his heart.

"I'm sorry, kiddo." The apology was brisk, and owned a gumshoe definitiveness.

"Are you sorry or just horny? I was trying to help."

"I'm really sorry. It hurts to not carry your share of the load." He put his face in his hands in a charade of grief, which easily became real. "Where do I meet him?"

"On the corner of Kolarik and 651. It seems a little mysterious but the meeting is supposed to be a secret."

"I'll get there. Somehow."

"Of course you will. It's only a few miles away. I'll have the newspaper and breakfast ready when you get back."

"I don't get why it's so fucking early in the morning."

"You used to get up at seven, darling. You come here now."

He collapsed at her knees with an "Oh Diana," shoving Hudley away with a foot. They embraced and he peeked down at her tits. A troubleshooter. Life was changing. He drew back and looked in her eyes. He was wedged between her legs which smelled like Nivea lotion.

"I think this might be your break, darling."

His head sunk to her partially exposed lap. Troubleshooter

had a good ring to it. He drew in his breath deeply; Nivea was tropical, reminding him of their trip to Florida and Nassau. In a way he was testing out his nose. He would be underspoken and witty in the morning. She slid the backs of her knees over his shoulders.

16

Someone yanked at his foot with a cool hand. Still within the grasp of sleep as he was, something stopped him from striking out with one of his not inconsiderable legs in the kind of heel-to-gut shot that can be fatal to all but the sturdiest enemies: an accurately propelled heel with two hundred pounds behind it can sink into a stomach until it blasts against the spine. An intestine bursts, spilling the acrid poison. There's a very good chance of peritonitis. In auto accidents it is listed under the euphemism of "internal injuries." It is the same method by which noble porpoises jelly the guts of marauding sharks, only they use their noses, lacking heels. The death that ensues is an accelerated form of rot and is not pretty. Luckily few know how to deliver the blow, or else no one would want to wake anyone up.

"Wake up. You can't be late."

"Uckfay ooyay," he muttered in childish pig Latin, a language that seems to have lost its cachet among the young.

"Come on, Johnny. Here's your juice."

He slid his hand up her nightie, slowly and tenderly grasping her as one does a bowling ball. She squirmed a little, then was still to avoid spilling the glass of cranberry juice, his private nostrum to prevent kidney stones. She bared her teeth, crossed her eyes, and hissed.

"Not now!"

"*Pourquoi, ma cul magnifique?*" His French was unerringly lacking in accuracy and grammar.

"Later, porky. I don't want one of your speed shots. When you get back, fine."

"Okay, if we can get really dirty and weird?"

"As dirty and weird as you want, darling."

In the car he reflected you invariably couldn't get as weird as a woman, once she really got cranked up. Once in New York he had bedded a ballerina who snorted great quantities of cocaine, a hard drug he wouldn't touch at gunpoint. The upshot of the night had been her insistence that he put a whole hand "in," as it were. Naturally he refused, on grounds that were listed, sententiously, under headings—impossible, scary, probable injuries, too weird. The ballerina then dropped three Quaaludes and went to sleep. Warlock had always felt that the drug of the young masses, marijuana, stole incentive, which anyway seemed in short supply. There were exceptions to its use though; in May he and Diana made a short trip to the Upper Peninsula to clear the marital air. The weather had been cold and rainy, forcing them out of their tent and into a shabby tourist cabin with the single beguiling feature of a Franklin stove. She had brought along a small stash of dope given her by one of those young doctors who look like they've just jumped out of a TV set. This particular batch proved hideously strong and made him horny as a billy goat so they made love repeatedly, listened without irony to the rain, built fires, made huge sandwiches out of the limited contents of their foam cooler. They drank lots of beer and bourbon, smoked huge bombers, endured the lukewarm waters and cold floor of the shower, and played absurdly adolescent sexual games. These wonderful renewals, he thought, these returns to a biologically drying spring. The tinge of the drag-ass entered again, and he dismissed it with vigor, stepping hard on the gas.

He pulled off on the shoulder of the gravel road, noting that there were no visible houses and he was ten minutes early. He felt butterflies fluttering in his stomach and there was that stern, hushed sense of getting ready for the Big Game. He craned his neck out the window, catching a glimpse of white at the top of an ash tree. Was it a sea gull from Lake Michigan or perhaps a very rare albino crow? The crow would indicate an omen. Warlock was steadfastly Christian without knowing it, and habitually pooh-poohed all notions of magic, witchcraft, ghosts and suchlike, which, since they could neither be proved or disproved, had been tossed from the church with Aristotelian disdain. He got out of the car but the bird was gone. It had rained in the night and he was careful not to muddy his spit-shined cordovans. He stared into a swale near the road, unable to deny that his body felt a dark sense of mystery and forboding. There was a black bird with red wings on a cattail which made it a red-winged black bird. He wasn't good at birds other than the basic crow, robin, blue jay, while Diana was a master with her Peterson guide. A grouse flushed thunderously from a covert of dogwood as he approached. He jumped straight up and came down gasping, his heart beating wildly. The fucking bird gave no warning. Just as suddenly a huge black BMW pulled up behind him, and he swung around as if to backhand the car. The car had silver reflector windows and Warlock couldn't see the driver. It must be Rabun, he thought.

The interview began awkwardly, with a barely audible Bach cantata on the tape deck. Warlock thought it unfortunate that they were dressed almost identically in blue blazers and chinos, but Rabun seemed not to notice. The difference was Rabun's dark, balloon shoes. The doctor had the resumé on his lap and was pouring two Bloody Marys from a thermos.

"I called Vergil Schmidt. We're old acquaintances, both thirty-second degree Masons. He spoke very highly of you."

"Thank you."

"Don't thank me. I didn't say it, Vergil did. The only real black mark on your resumé is your divorce. I'm essentially Catholic and despise divorce."

"I thought you said you were a Mason. Masons are Protestant." Warlock wasn't going to be driven into a corner so early in the interview.

"Very smart. I planted that to see if you were rehearsing or listening. Besides, your first wife spoke highly of you." Rabun drank deeply from his Bloody Mary.

"Thank you."

"Stop it for Christ's sake. I'm scarcely Marilyn. I haven't complimented you."

"Excuse me. I'm a little rattled."

"I know adrenaline. I saw the grouse flush. And you wonder why we're meeting here?"

"Of course. It's a little odd."

"I don't like people getting the whole picture on me. I'm an inventor. Inventors are secretive in order to prevent some swine from stealing their inventions. More than the money, I want sole credit for my ideas. I am not by nature a collaborator."

"Yes, sir. Inventors are temperamentally similar to artists. They don't want someone else to sign their paintings."

"Excellent! Diana insisted that you were bright."

"Thank you."

Rabun looked at him with amazement, then both chuckled at the gaff. Warlock was beginning to admire the man. Rabun suddenly beeped at a fledgling bird sitting on his hood ornament, then smiled cynically.

"Best the little bugger learn about technology. . . . So my problem is this. I make a great deal of money and I have diversified my holdings through the usual assortment of middlemen, CPA's, lawyers, bank officers, investment counselors, realtors. I'm a little eccentric and these feebleminded middle management types like to swindle people like myself. They think I'm otherworldly, missing the point that I'm the one that made the dough. My wife is in Florida on a semipermanent basis and is obviously supporting a gaggle of leeches. My son's down there and is probably a homosexual though I haven't confirmed this. I have reason to suspect he's being swindled." Rabun buried his face in his hands and sighed.

"I'm sorry that things are going badly, sir." He felt poignantly the sorrow of the old man, and was reminded of the beleaguered Gauguin in Tahiti.

"Thank you. The point is that something can be done about the whole thing." Rabun stared at him darkly then reached over into the back seat and withdrew a large briefcase. "Guard this with your life. Read its contents. I must swear you to total secrecy. For instance I have extensive landholdings in the

Upper Peninsula. I'm sure the local dolts are stealing my timber. It doesn't amount to a great deal of money but I don't like to be cheated. We'll meet on Tuesday for lunch. Read it closely, give me some ideas."

"I don't quite understand my place in this whole thing." Warlock felt himself gradually merging with a larger scheme of affairs.

"I need a troubleshooter, an undercover man, a sort of glorified private detective with your kind of background. Don't give me your answer now." Rabun raised his hand to quell Warlock's eagerness. "Absolute secrecy. Not even your wife, kind soul that she is. Swear it."

"I swear it, sir."

17

"Let's face it, my life is changed," he said to himself, on the way home. The blue sky with knots of cumuli, the green hills and the green lake beyond, even the gravel rattling under the bumpers seemed exuberant. He tried to sing Jerry Lee Lewis's "Chantilly Lace," muffed it, but still burbled along to the melody. When he turned onto Eagle Highway, however, there was a stomach-hollowing wave of déjà vu waiting for him. The car slowed to a creep and a string of Catholics returning from mass beeped. Fuck you. Of course! He'd been following the same route that fatal morning nearly a month before when after the oracular dream he had vowed to change his future. His eyes moistened with this epiphany. His heart actually swelled and that lump that defies cynicism rose in the throat. Perhaps the lump was the stuff of life itself, he pondered. He conjured up a savage lust for life and love and slammed the car into first. He nearly growled.

Diana fixed him a cheddar and bacon omelet, a hair less runny than he preferred. The Sunday paper was beside his plate, and the secret briefcase. They had barely spoken in the ten minutes or so since his return. The trouble in paradise had begun when he'd hefted the weighty briefcase out of the car. In a way it held two destinies, he thought. Jesus, he better play it smart. Even more troublesome was that he could share nothing with his beloved; neither the secret of his own radical change nor the secret represented by the briefcase.

"Can't you say anything, darling? Did it go badly?" She massaged his neck and shoulders while he ate desultorily.

"It went well. We liked each other. I seem to have a job."

"What exactly is the job?"

"I'm sorry but I can't say."

"Oh for god's sake, you can tell me. You're the one who can't keep a secret."

"I can't tell anyone. I have to keep this secret."

"What's the briefcase gripped between your feet?"

"Please, Diana. I can't talk about it."

"What's to prevent me from peeking at it when you're asleep or on the toilet?"

"I'll take it with me."

"I'm jealous. Now you're going to fuck a briefcase." She laughed in her teasing way with a fleck of the frosting of the sweet roll she was eating stuck to her upper lip. She was still wearing her nightie, and without undies.

"It's not funny, Diana. This is extremely serious business. I've sworn . . ."

"Oh stop it. Who gives a fuck about the briefcase. I can tease."

"You sure can."

"I thought we were going to be weird when you got home." She took a joint from the cupboard, lit it, and inhaled deeply. She passed it to him.

"Nothing doing. I got a lot of material to bone up on by Tuesday."

"You're turning me down for the first time." She pretended to be grieved.

"Not exactly. I just don't want to get stoned."

"I sort of thought you'd make yourself up like a Negro. I was all ready for you to be a Negro."

The fact was that on two occasions he had worn blackface and they had had a splendid time. Unfortunately he had neglected the base for the makeup on both occasions and it was a bitch to get off. It left his eyes pink and his skin raw.

"I don't feel like being a Negro today. I have too much on my mind."

"Okay, I know you do and I'm happy for your job. Let's settle for the tuxedo." She sat down on the chair near the window and hugged her knees. Despite his preoccupation with the Rabun business, his wiener began to swirl in his trousers at the sight of her underthighs and discrete thatch, nestled there like a thrush, nest and all.

"So it's the tuxedo on Sunday." He rose and thrust the briefcase into the refrigerator.

"Why the refrigerator. Are you nuts?"

"In house fires, excepting those of extreme nature, the contents of the refrigerator are rarely disturbed."

The scenario of the tuxedo was solid, but scarcely as electric as the fresher Negro. Warlock was a high-class swell arriving at an extremely expensive whorehouse. Diana was a demure country girl on her first day on the job, and wearing only a satin slip he had purchased in an antique clothing shop in New York. They would dance, at first stiffly, then tenderly, to a Frank Sinatra album. Then he would pretend to be drunk and begin mauling her, at which she would weep. He then, with unbridled sensuality, would guide her to an armchair over whose arms her lovely legs would eventually settle. It went on from there at some length, depending on their energies. On this particular Sunday hers exceeded his by several fathoms. He was ransomed by a loud knock at the door which sent Diana wobbling to the bedroom. He zipped up and measured his tread, slicking back his hair.

It was Clete and his wife La Verne. He waved at them through the oval window of the door, neglecting to open it. Somewhere in his brain there was still a jackhammer in operation. He remembered that he had invited them over to barbecue something. Rather than prolong the inane gaze, Clete opened the door.

"Having a dance?" Clete asked, noting the tuxedo. He was carrying a large package. La Verne looked around with amused suspiciousness. She knew that everyone was odd and did not particularly question it.

"You might say that. I got a job." Warlock followed them into the kitchen.

"Doing what?" Clete tried to open the refrigerator.

"Stop!" Warlock grabbed his arm, a rhinestone cuff link clacking against the door. "I'm sorry. I guess it's okay."

Clete had jumped back so Warlock opened the door and slid in the packages, but La Verne had craned her neck around the door.

"What the hell is that briefcase in the refrigerator for?" She laughed.

"I'm afraid it has to be a secret. It's connected with the job."

"You've turned into a goofy fucker," Clete said, tearing the door from Warlock's grasp and taking a beer. "We can go home."

"Don't be silly." Diana came into the kitchen in a bathrobe and gave Clete a vampy hug. "He's become a spy or something. What'd you bring? I'm hungry."

"Got some steaks. Slaughtered a steer last week. And what's left of the white morels. They're dry."

"Oh goody." She kissed him smack on the lips, not having lost her heat. La Verne looked out the window.

"I guess I better change." Warlock was flustered and wondered if taking off the tuxedo might help.

"You look like James Bond," La Verne said.

"In a pig's ass." Clete grabbed his lapels. "If you're really a spy why does Asshollah still have the hostages?"

"He's an old man. He doesn't know what to do." Warlock took a bottle of whiskey from the counter and swigged deeply as a solution to a problem that didn't exist.

"Now he's Johnny again." LaVerne said passing the bottle to Clete. "He'll never change. He's our penguin."

18

He awoke late in the evening, hearing Boccherini from the living room, and the popping and cracking of his hangover between his ears. His right ear was still ringing but that was the aftereffect of firing the pistol and could not be blamed on whiskey. What had begun as a gentle Sunday barbecue had progressed into a celebration of his employment. Now there was a tremor of worry that the job hadn't been specifically offered, but he recognized this doubt was physiological, the down side of whiskey. The Boccherini was helping everything but his thirst; the music reminded him of a Romeo and Juliet movie filmed in Verona, with all those old buildings and beautiful costumes. He had wept at the ending and for once Diana hadn't felt the whole thing gauche and sentimental. He had thought the dialogue was great, though a little hard to follow, then remembered Shakespeare had written it.

He made his coffee clumsily, noticing with delight that he hadn't read the Sunday *Free Press,* which lay fresh and virginal except the sports page. He plucked at his sore ear. Cletis had thought, after a number of drinks, that Warlock needed side-arm training. They had shot at a large oil can and Warlock was pleased to hit it three out of ten, though Clete's score was perfect.

"That's not too bad for me. I mean a human is bigger than a can," Warlock had said.

"Bullshit. That means you'll die seven out of ten times, and an attacker moves a little better than an oil can."

"Maybe I'd better practice. Actually, I'm more a private detective than a spy, to be frank."

"I already knew you wasn't a spy."

"How come?"

"A true spy never admits he's a spy, even to his wife or best friend."

After they had fired the last round Warlock had allowed Hudley to run out and shake the can with vigor to make sure it was dead. The dog had cut its lip and sucked on the slight wound with a certain appetite. This temporarily disturbed his gastric system, but they proceeded happily through porterhouses, and the morels Warlock had soaked, then sautéed with shallots.

He hurried through the newspaper when he remembered the briefcase sheltered in the fireproof refrigerator. There was a minor betrayal of trust incorporated in his tuxedo, fandango, and booze-soaked sleep. Anyone could have sneaked in the back porch and slipped out with a very cold briefcase. Jesus. Get back on your toes. Attention! He lashed cold water in his face, slapped himself a little too firmly, then set up a card table in the living room so he could see the Sunday night CBS news with Ed Bradley while studying the portfolio. Diana was asleep on the couch, and her robe had edged up her legs to a distracting degree so he took a quick peek—still there—and pulled the robe down gently to a decent level. His pulse beat wildly as he pressed the latch on the briefcase, as if he expected a bomb, a cobra, a cuckoo clock.

First of all the papers were very cold and there weren't quite as many of them as he had expected. Much of the bulk of the briefcase was made up of three books: Schlinkert's *Modern Investigative Techniques*, a lawyer's manual on federal income tax regulations, and a popular title on business crime in paperback. I can't read all this shit before Tuesday, he thought, like a complaining sophomore. The business crime title had the attraction of a florid cover with a bikini-clad floozy sitting on a tycoon's lap. The tycoon smoked a stogie with a blurred grin and one of the girl's thighs was out of proportion, Warlock saw with his artist's eye. The first folder contained the sort of holdings he was familiar with through the foundation, mostly in a revokable trust agreement with a large bank in New York. Why not Detroit, he wondered? There were a few millions in ordinary blue chips, and an additional smaller folder carrying Rabun's active trading account with E. F. Hutton, plus three hundred grand in their Money Management Fund, the limit, Warlock recognized. There were also several pages containing a series of orthodox tax shelters, and crypto-tax-dodge delayed retirement funds.

It was the second folder marked Private Holdings that held the surprises, a CPA's nightmare, a mishmash of smaller venture schemes including timberlands in the Upper Peninsula, a shipping pallet manufacturing company, thirty percent of Vergil's think tank, three motels, half of a marina on Singer Island, more than half of a weight reduction clinic in West Palm Beach, half a Ford garage in Kansas that named another Rabun as copartner. Toward the end of the folder the holdings diminished in Rabun's share. At the end was a sucker-punch note from the good doctor. "Don't be discouraged. Lunch at my house at noon, Tuesday. May I have a page, double spaced, of your insights?"

Warlock turned as Diana yawned and stretched. He had missed Ed Bradley and was pissed. Sunday night TV was a wasteland of evangelism in Northern Michigan—Jim Bakker's PTL club on one station and Jack Van Impe with his wife Rexella on the other station. And the country music station signed off at eleven P.M. Lately he had begun to listen to this mordant, somber music for the first time since he had been stationed in El Paso. It seemed to focus on some of his problems, singing as it often did of the camaraderie of outcasts, drinkers, adulterers, the unemployed, the peripheral whites far from the centers of wealth and power, much less solvency. There was a horrifying song by Merle Haggard about some young fool turning twenty-one in prison and doing life without parole. He could not imagine a worse fate, knowing through his father how men behaved in prisons. Diana had thought his TV crush on Dolly Parton to be laughable. Clete loved her, too, referring to her as Miss Dolly, as they listened to albums of her crystal Appalachian voice, singing of woes more real than their own. Now that he had a job perhaps he should stop listening to such music? Bad luck is self-fulfilling prophesy, his mother always said. He felt Diana's breath on his ear and he slumped over to protect the papers from her sight.

"I'm sorry," he said.

"Must be important. You missed the news. I'm going to bed."

"Good night, darling."

"How can you kiss me when you're flopped over the table?" she teased.

"Just step back seven paces and I'll tuck you in."

She counted off the steps drowsily while he shuffled the papers into a pile. He embraced her and directed her toward the bedroom, but she slid a hand in his robe and massaged his weenie.

"Just one little secret?"

"Not even for the dread Swedish ice-cube trick."

She crawled in bed and wagged her hinder at him and Warlock thought of slipping her a phony secret in return for something odd, but a shadow crossed over her fair brow.

"Johnny, don't take the job unless you really want it. We're living fine on what I make."

"Don't be silly. I want the job. It's suited to my talent. I want it badly and I don't even know what I'm going to get paid."

"I worry about you. You drink so much more than you used to. You watch TV until it drives me nuts. We used to read together."

"I know it. But I feel I'm getting it together now." He sat on the bed beside her and caressed her neck.

"I worried when I saw that briefcase because you were always so charming, so good at the general picture but you didn't do well at the details. A few nights ago you were watching Johnny Carson. I watched you flipping a coin until my feet got tired."

"It was just curiosity." Which was the truth. A hundred flips turned up fifty-three to forty-seven. He also remarked on the exact time he went to bed every night, right down to the last digit of his digital watch, 12:11:37 and time to turn in.

"I love you and want you to have a good life. Good night."
She embraced him.

"I think I got a handle on it," he said at the door. "I'm
changing it in a lot of ways. Good night."

He went to the refrigerator and picked at the ample amount
of rare meat Diana and La Verne had left on their steak bones,
washing it down with a cold Stroh's. He felt the solid, adven-
turous clarity of a trapper setting off into the mountains, an
unknown vastness, for another season.

19

On Tuesday morning he awoke to one of those totally grim thunderstorms that wrack the Midwest in the summer; the windowpanes of the old farmhouse rattled, the bedroom walls lit up bluish with the closer strokes of lightning, and Hudley howled under the bed—not so much a howl really as an endlessly protracted moan interrupted by gulps of air. The dog didn't howl in thunderstorms when Diana was there to hold a paw and stroke his grizzled head. Warlock reflected that in his own childhood his mom had been definitely more comforting than his dad during thunderstorms; his dad, in fact, would say "That's God barking at you for being such a miserable little pissant."

The dog drove him to the kitchen without anger—his own fears were far ranging: fire, the dark, people with one eye, people with goiters, tall blacks, homosexuals, generals, school principals, priests, Lutheran ministers, airplanes, drop forges, fast drivers, sexually aggressive women, large Japanese, psychiatrists, cancer, cheating wives, fistfights, death. In that his father had always been a policeman he did not fear the law. You have nothing to fear from the law if you don't break it, was a truism he had been raised on. He grew up with a definite wariness of shifty eyed people who might try to hurt his father.

He pushed aside the fat, fresh *Free Press* with scorn. Fat papers for fat, slack minds. He drew out of his briefcase the single page of terse clean prose he would pass on to Rabun. It seemed too bold in the light of the natural conservatism of morning: while composing it the night before his mind was cold and strident, but now he missed all the emotional connectives. What the fuck. It was too late now. He had barely enough time to shower and shave before dressing for lunch. What appeared now as a sore point was in the last paragraph of the memo. He had begun by complimenting the doctor on the wisdom of the choices in the core of his portfolio. Then he went off on a meandering tangent that centered on fat as a metaphor: the doctor's "personal holdings" were likened to a mass of inefficient fat on a body, and so on. Warlock was the man to pare the fat. He concluded that his salary be paid against a recovery fee of twenty percent of pretax profits. This followed the obvious notion that books were easily jimmied and a CPA could only deal with the figures given him. How could Rabun determine the actual number of people who actually stayed in his motels, how many people visited his fat clinic, how many boats were stored at the marina? There was room at the bottom of both copies of the memo for their signatures. God, how dare I, he thought with blood rushing to his face. The problem had to be the three whiskeys. Just before he went to college Dad had taken him out to the garage with a six-pack of beer. There were a lot of flies in the garage and Warlock had been instructed to catch five flies with a hand then chugalug a beer. He did both with grace. The second five flies were a little harder but the beer went down easy. At the end of an hour, and the six-pack, he felt like puking and couldn't catch a single fly. His father, a steady drinker himself, marched off without a word after this curiously Oriental lesson. Warlock had stood leaning dizzily against the workbench thinking, who the fuck wants to catch flies anyhow? What do they make flyswatters or fly sticky strips for? I'm going over to Marcia's and show her and her sister the old what for by god. Marcia's burly father, a rural milkman, had immediately tossed him out of the house and called his parents. He puked on their lawn, more in sickness than in vengeance.

Diana had gone to a movie with Gretchen to leave Warlock free for his evening's work. She had rather cutely put a note in the refrigerator—"Finish your work before you snack. Eating makes you sleepy. I love you. Good luck." Quite a girl. The new job would enable them to travel again. Perhaps Venice next spring. She had this nasty ambition to travel up the Amazon but big snakes were major on his fear list.

After the first draft of the memo he had called his dad to share the good news about his job. The call had gone well until he announced that he was going to be "sort of a detective."

"Oh Jesus no. I order you to quit before you start."

"I can't do that. I need a job and anyhow, why?"

"Here I am watching a baseball game. Right? Then you say detective. Baseball bores the shit out of me. I can't wait until September. This Garagiola guy is a real numb-nuts. You're just not the right type for detective work. You're too bighearted and you don't notice anything. You'll get your ass kicked. Get some office job. Christ, you got two degrees. Do you think I'd be knocking heads if I had two degrees?"

"I don't know, Dad. I had hoped you'd be pleased for Diana and me."

"Please don't get me wrong, Johnny. Here the other night this boonie shoots a grocer in the fucking face with a twelve gauge. I'm there afterwards looking it over and I step on something. What is it?"

"I don't know, Dad."

"Of course you don't. It was three teeth still hooked together by a piece of gum and jawbone. I almost lost my cookies. I had just eaten Myrna's special old country goulash."

"But Dad, this is just business crime. A lot of people are swindling this millionaire doctor."

"I never knew a doctor that wasn't a fucking swindler. A lot of them take dope."

"Not this guy. He's a brilliant inventor doctor."

"Okay, okay. You're forty-one. It's your business."

"Forty-two."

"Okay. Just remember a few things. I've got some theories from four decades of police business. So listen. Number one, everyone is a criminal. That's because the world is a crime. It might somehow be tied to religion. I haven't figured it all out, like if it's tied into our fall from grace and that shit."

"Jesus, Dad. Diana and me aren't criminals. Mom wasn't. She had a heart of gold."

"Look into your heart, son. Your mom was a spitfire when we were first married. And Diana is too beautiful to trust."

"God, Dad, you're really pissing in the whiskey. I just called with a little good news for a change."

"I don't mean they're criminal criminals. Look into your own heart. Look at god's law and the Sermon on the Mount and all that shit. I'm talking theory. I mean I've always committed adultery and thought about killing people I hated."

"I see what you mean. Man is doomed unless he improves his nature."

"Don't give me that liberal shit. You pussies all live in fur-lined closets. Get out on the street and take a look. First of all get Clete to teach you how to shoot a pistol. . . ."

"We started yesterday. . . ."

"Great. Maybe you're getting smarter. Get a heavy punching bag and work out. Don't drink on the job. And remember everyone, I mean everyone, is trying to fuck you over in one way or another. From kids to grocers to wives to bosses. Even dogs. Get it?"

"I understand. Be on your toes. Be wary."

"Right. And call me if you get in trouble. I still got a lot of connections in Michigan. I'll send you a secret card to carry. Our kind stick together. And you know what?"

"What?"

"Detroit never should have traded LeFlore to Montreal. Sportswise Detroit has all the hicks running teams. Look at the Pistons. Look at the Red Wings. Look at the Lions."

"I agree."

"I love you, son."

After recovering from the initial shock of the phone call he rewrote the memo with a fresh, icy eye. He was forced to retype it having put the carbon paper in backwards. By the time Diana got home he felt sullen, cynical, but somehow with a sense of firm, unshakable control. He smoked a cigarette without taking it from his mouth as she talked about the movie. He only picked at the cold cuts. He would become lean. He asked her with a new and certain firmness to undress and put on her nightgown in front of him.

"I think it's going to be good, kid."

"What's going to be good?"

"All of it."

20

He was early so he pulled off the road within a mile of Rabun's:
Diana's map was precise though her sole visit had been at
night. Now he breathed deeply and closed his eyes in order to
manufacture some quick composure. At least a dollop. A *soupçon* would do, or a mite, a mote. Nothing there but whirling
and rehearsals, the raw material of nightmares. All this thinking ahead wasn't doing him much good. Diana teased him
about his penchant for sitting in a corner and "thinking things
over." She insisted that he was rehearsing his life so much that
he had no time to live it. There were even postrehearsals after
marital arguments when he would restructure the scenario
until he was either right, or his retreat was dignified. Now there
was the vertigo of dreams sitting on a country road and everyone knows that dreams and nightmares are bottomless: no
earth beneath the feet, no floors. He grabbed at the inside
rearview mirror to look at himself but his hand trembled and
it was difficult to find himself for a few moments. His father
was right. He didn't know shit about being a detective. He
rarely read mysteries. Carolyn Keene's *Clue of the Dancing*

Puppet came to mind. When he was twelve or so his aunt had given him a box of Nancy Drew mysteries. Nancy was smart as a whip. Dancing puppet, indeed; amateur puppeteers and public whistlers were high on his shit list.

Rabun's house was impressive on the outside though a bit too Bauhaus for his own taste. There was the additional oddity that the house simply appeared in the forest at the end of a long driveway; there was no lawn and a large tree grew precipitously close to the roof. Two huge dogs Warlock recognized as rottweilers were romping on the lawn. They were immediately not interested in his getting out of the car. He rolled up the window in alarm. Other people's big dogs were on the fear list. Rabun walked around the corner in his balloon boots and blew a silent, high frequency dog whistle and the rottweilers scooted to his side. Warlock approached gingerly with his eyes averted. Rabun mumbled in German and offered him two dog biscuits that he nearly ate in his confusion.

"Say *mein liebchen, mein edelweiss* and give them the biscuits."

Warlock did so and the curs jumped him lovingly, licking his sport coat and hands. One ran off and brought him a putrid muskrat head to toss.

"They're true *Schutz* hounds from the Cologne area," Rabun said with pride.

"I thought they were rottweilers."

" '*Schutz*' is a type of prolonged training. They obey hundreds of voice commands. I want them to know you for obvious reasons. You're always completely safe here until eleven o'clock at which point a buzzer goes off. Then no one is safe until seven in the morning when the buzzer goes off again."

"How about you?"

"Don't be silly. I'm their god. I could strangle them and they wouldn't complain."

"Makes you think, doesn't it?" Warlock was swept away in dark religious conclusions.

"No. Not in the least. Dogs don't make me think. Except about other dogs. The dogs of my life. That sort of thing."

Lunch was one of the most splendid of his life, Warlock felt, a little dreamily. An entire bottle of a Bordeaux, a Beychevelle '67, had soothed his frayed synapses. Diana had told Rabun of the joy Warlock had experienced in London and there was an array of English dishes including a steak and oyster pie, a mixed grill including a broiled kidney, a pork cutlet, lamb chop, bacon, a woodcock of all things, a broiled stuffed tomato and a side of fresh spinach. Warlock's heart went out to the doctor who ate a bowl of stewed millet and ice water.

"The boobs at the Mayo Clinic tell me I have the worst gout they've ever seen. It's been controlled by allopurinol but I'm only able to dine twice a week at most. Or I suffer terribly. I've become so cranky about it over the past decade my wife has taken to living in Florida."

"I feel awful eating this in front of you."

"Don't be stupid. I ordered the meal. Ten years ago I weighed nearly three hundred and now I weight one fifty. I'm in my sixties but I fully recaptured my sex life. Gluttons are traditionally bad fucks. Balzac and Rasputin were exceptions."

"It's best to keep in shape for the sack," Warlock agreed.

"Not very elegantly put, but true." Rabun suddenly threw his porridge spoon at Warlock's head.

"Jesus!" He snatched the spoon out of the air a foot in front of his face.

"Just testing your alertness. Very good."

While Warlock had his blackberry torte, demitasse, and Hine cognac, Rabun studied the memo, his pen poised over it like a bird of prey. He scratched a few times, added his signature to both copies, and pushed them back to Warlock.

"Very good. I knocked the commission down to seventeen and a half to appear better at business than I am. I'll start you at forty-five, your last inflated salary for putting the feeble, the lame, the dolts, on the dole."

"Don't start me there if you feel it's inflated," Warlock paused with dignity, a spoonful of torte on the verge of his lips.

"You're being baroque again. I wouldn't hire anyone willing to go backwards. Time moves forward quickly in twenty-four hour segments. So does life, unfortunately for the aged. We'll start with a one year contract. Strictly cash. I think absolute secrecy should be our central working point."

"I agree, sir."

"Sir is not necessary. Call me Doctor Rabun."

"Fine by me, Doctor Rabun."

They toured the laboratory which was somewhat of a disappointment to Warlock who owned a horror and science fiction notion of science. The door had been thrilling, opening at the wave of a ring on Rabun's hand, affixed tightly below a knuckle and which could not be removed without cutting off a finger. But inside there was virtually nothing in the large, white, windowless room. All the paraphernalia was evidently locked in a wall of stainless steel cabinets. There was a long table with drawers and another examining table with stirrups, with a tall stool beside it.

"Diana has probably told you what I'm known for. Mainly

kidney pumps, surgical equipment, shoes, prosthetic devices of various sorts. When I need complicated equipment I use Vergil's lab in East Lansing."

"Yes, sir."

"Doctor Rabun. Let's just make it Rabun."

"Rabun."

The doctor then offered a bit of a shock, though Warlock kept his composure as Rabun waved his ring before a drawer revealing a tray of what certainly looked like dildos. They were a livid though realistic pink and came in a half a dozen sizes.

"We need a little levity. Pick one of them up."

"This is embarrassing." Warlock picked one out of the middle rather diplomatically. It began vibrating and turning warm —too utterly lifelike—and he dropped it to the floor in alarm.

"Don't drop it, you oaf. It's priceless." Rabun shrieked with laughter. Warlock picked it up, but it pulsed and he held it shyly. Rabun, still laughing, took a small black bar from his pocket resembling a remote TV tuner or a pocket computer. "I've imitated here the shimmying of a porpoise's skin as it moves through the water. The physiologically impotent stick their penises in and they are grasped. Then they punch the controls for the desired effect."

"Marvelous." Warlock replaced the object with distaste.

"They'll be marketed this fall at five grand a shot. I deserve the Nobel but it's never given to a pragmatic genius."

21

By the end of the afternoon they were cronies, or so Warlock thought on the way home, neglecting his father's admonition against trust. He anyway found his father's language and attitudes more than a little embarrassing for the same reason he found Kojak to be a bore and a dingo. It was the tough guy charade, the bartender and cab driver nonsense of having all the angles covered. He knew he could trust his father, Diana and Rabun. He patted his sport coat pocket where an envelope held four thousand dollars, a month's pay in advance plus expense money. Unfortunately the money caused a niggling fear: Rabun had demanded a promise that Warlock wouldn't file on the money; even the IRS shouldn't know what they were up to. He had always paid every iota he owed the IRS, more out of patriotism than fear. In the ensuing conversation Rabun had been excessively cynical.

"This is upsetting. I've always paid my taxes."

"I'm audited quarterly. It's impossible. Don't be a moron. Nothing can be traced."

"It always seemed to me that an essential part of the social contract was that everyone kicked in his fair share," Warlock had replied.

"A charming notion. Perhaps we can get you a suit tailored out of the flag, or a job as a boy scout leader."

"I was an Eagle by sixteen." Warlock's mind wandered back to the ceremony.

"No doubt. My taxes already cover the salaries of ten senators. I find this unbearable. Where are Robert Taft and Arthur Vandenberg when we need them? Dead."

"I could use that extra thirty percent for a nest egg. To be frank, my savings are nil."

"And you're depriving the government of a minor amount with which they would create more mischief."

"I suspect you're far to the right. I feel Reagan is wrong-headed and a little frightening to imagine in the arena of international politics."

"No. I consider myself a Jeffersonian. I'm so far left that I might be considered a rightist. I believe in pure research and privacy. Most of those you think of as the Right are fatuous business toadies, ignorant of history. The Left plays pocket pool with billions out of sentiment. Read Tolstoy."

When he pulled into the yard he noticed Diana dozing on a lawn chair in the warm, late afternoon sun. She wore a pale tan Brazilian string bikini that seemed a bit too flesh colored to wear in public, but he had long since given up advising her on matters of wardrobe. She woke as Hudley stood barking at the master for no particular reason except that he always did so.

"You're late. I almost called thinking you might have forgotten Ed and Sheila are coming over for dinner."

"I didn't forget," he lied. "What are we having?"

"I didn't want to go to the store and miss the sun so I made spaghetti sauce."

"Did you forget the basil?"

"How could I forget the basil when I'm married to you?" For a farm girl Diana was a surprisingly nonchalant cook. Spice racks in the Midwest, until lately, had not held the bounty of those in the East and West.

"I wish they weren't coming. I'm tired." He flopped down on the grass and tickled her bottom up through the mesh of the chair, scenting the cocoa butter she had rubbed on herself. He worked a forefinger under the edge of her bikini. Wrong place.

"How did it go?"

"Fine. I like the idea of working for a genius. I have to go to the Upper Peninsula tomorrow for a few days."

"Why?"

"You know I can't say why precisely. Let's just call it lumber."

She wriggled off his forefinger angrily. "You're carrying this bullshit secrecy to an absurd length."

"It's just part of the territory, darling. I'm sorry." He stood there, taking out the envelope and dropping its forty C-notes on her bare moist tummy. "Got some work to do."

After a shower and checking out Diana's distinctly mediocre spaghetti sauce (sneaking in a few cloves of garlic), he studied the folder and plat book maps of Rabun's timber holdings. There were two thousand irregularly shaped acres near Cape Sable in a totally unpopulated area of Luce County. The maps confused him so he called Clete. He wished he hadn't jauntily assured Rabun that he would walk the perimeters of the property to check out any timber stealing incursions.

"Clete. Johnny here. I got to walk off two thousand acres in the U.P. and I can't figure out the maps. I mean in a woods how do you find the boundaries?"

"Surveyor stakes."

"Steaks?" Sunday's porterhouses had been great.

"Surveyor's markers. Do you have the legal description of the land?"

"Yeah. It goes on for three pages."

"You can't walk two thousand acres in one day. It's eight miles and you don't know what the fuck you're doing."

"Thanks."

"Friends you tell. Everyone else you let get lost."

He had been tempted to pay Clete amply out of his expense money to go along as a guide, but he sensed his first trip on the job should be solo. Sink or swim.

"If you're such a great detective where did I hide the dough?" Diana had sneaked up behind him.

"Elementary, sugar." He peeked behind her ears, under her hair, down the bra of the bikini, then stripped down the bottoms that covered a rather male bulge. "Eureka!"

"Be gentle with me," she whispered with civic players intonations.

The dinner with Ed and Sheila was a decided flop. A day of overeating and work made him exhausted, and a few drinks added a certain gumshoe sense of the laconic to his attitude. The two couples had played bridge, dined, picnicked together, and Warlock had enjoyed them in a minimal fashion. The problem was that Ed and Sheila had just returned from a nine day est session in Chicago and their eyes, blazing with the newfound light, repelled him.

"I'm no longer going to try to dominate Ed in the sack," Sheila had announced, sucking in a stray noodle. "You know

I'd never blow him on a day he drank too much. Now we're just balling, true and free."

He noted the manner in which Ed had nodded smugly. The word "ball" always embarrassed Warlock, somehow connoting naked women fooling grotesquely with bowling balls, though not necessarily in a bowling alley.

"Werner showed me how my drinking was a cop-out on the real me inside." Ed pronounced Werner as in Vernor's ginger ale. He seemed to pig down the cheapish jug Burgundy like the old Ed.

Warlock mentioned that he had read in *People* that Werner's name used to be Jack Rosenburg and that Jews should be proud of their race and not change their names. Look at Einstein, Oppenheimer and Linus Pauling.

"I don't think Linus Pauling is Jewish," Diana said.

"The exception proves the rule." Warlock was bored and wanted to go to bed.

"You're a naysayer, Johnny, that's why you don't have a job."

"I have a job at triple what you make, fuckface. I think I'll change my name to Woody Jesus. Woody Allen is funny and I was raised on Jesus."

"You rubbed your boner against me two weeks ago," Sheila challenged, to everyone's amazement.

"I was thinking of Mrs. Carter," Warlock replied.

PART TWO

There is an imagination below the earth that abounds in animal forms, that revels and makes music.

JAMES HILLMAN
The Dream and the Underworld

22

Up North! Into the vastness, the wilderness, the unknown. By the time Warlock reached the Straits of Mackinac, and the bridge that separates the Upper Peninsula from lower Michigan, his adrenals were pumping fire and his heart soared. Perhaps his whole life had been a preparation for this summer when life, which had so apparently abandoned him, now lifted him up, took him to herself, renewed and ready for action. He felt himself totally salvaged by the baptism of his dream the month before. He had grasped the future like a chalice, pursued it as a knight setting off for Jerusalem through the dank forests of Europe, and down through Turkey to the burning sands of the Middle East, where he no doubt swapped his cumbersome horse for a camel. The immense Mackinac Bridge itself, which ordinarily made him slouch down in the seat with vertigo, now gleamed like a path over some sort of holy Rubicon. He did not know that the bridge of dreams is the bridge downward, and that in entering this terrain of sleep he had ruffled the ghastly feathers of the strange gods.

At the tollbooth on the far side of the bridge Hudley lunged and snapped at the toll taker when he handed back the change. When Warlock leaned far over to slug the dog in the back seat his .38 dropped out of the shoulder holster. Luckily the toll taker hadn't noticed. He had a sport license for the pistol, rather than a concealed weapons permit, and Michigan authorities were harsh on such details. But it had been pleasant in the morning strapping the pistol on over a lightweight wool shirt and looking at himself in the mirror with his legs slightly splayed in the manner of Marines. Chinos, boots, an Abercrombie & Fitch cotton safari jacket completed the costume. There had been a brief tingle of the ludicrous driving down through Leelanau County thusly armed. The whole area was virtually free of any crimes of violence and had always been so. "A murder every ten years," was a local quip.

He pulled off into a rest area to hide the gun and take off the jacket which made him wilt in the heat. Hudley had been whining to pee for quite some time. There was a surge of anger over having to haul the fucking dog along. They had stupidly forgotten to reserve kennel space and a long Fourth of July weekend was coming up, with vacationers' pets taking all the space. Diana intended to spend several evenings and nights in Traverse City planning a feminist newsletter with her friends. He acceded to taking the dog along after a brief fantasy about getting lost and having Hudley lope into the circle of light the campfire cast carrying a young deer. He would spear chunks of deer meat with a green stick and roast it over the fire. There wouldn't be any salt and pepper but salt was bad for his borderline high blood pressure. The dog would keep him warm and lead him out of the forest at dawn.

Now, unfortunately, the dog had completed his peeing, and raced past his master, chasing a noisome semitruck down the highway.

"Biscuit, biscuit, biscuit, biscuit," Warlock yelled. The dog swerved and trotted back, jumping into the car.

"Tough shit. It was a sucker shot. I forgot the biscuits."

They drove on with the memory of the roasting meat causing him discomfort. Diana had packed him a large cellophane sack full of dried fruit and nuts after he had announced at breakfast that the trip would be a fine shot at losing a few pounds. It was a severe understatement to call Michigan a culinary wasteland the further north you traveled. Once on a fishing trip with Clete, Warlock had been served a bright yellow chicken gravy on a slab of gray roast beef. With the advent of the microwave ovens he suspected that many of the mom and pop operations rarely cooked, only reheated. He revered the words of an old Jewish literature professor who said the downfall of a nation could be detected in the misuse of language by its public officials, and the disintegration of its eating habits.

He tried a handful of Diana's health mix, averting his eyes from the highway to spot a cashew, a morsel of pecan, a dried apricot and something rather amorphous nestled in a cup of sunflower seeds in his palm. The chewing was a bit difficult but there was a sense of instantly losing weight, however short-lived. A few moments later he swerved into the parking lot of a small restaurant called the Rathskeller. There were no trucks in the parking lot, a good sign, he thought. And only one car, which made it iffy.

The three hours it took to drive from the restaurant to Grand Marais, a small fishing village on Lake Superior, were spent unpleasantly trying to digest a platter of sauerbraten, spätzle and red cabbage. The food was good, but not good driving food, much less secret mission food: his eyelids drooped and itched for sleep, the soaring heart became a fat hen at roost. Many of the problems the world has had with Germany in the past century, he felt, could be traced to this leaden, fascistic diet. It sucked out the aerial spirit and made one fart and feel unkind. He possessed enough self-knowledge, though, to avoid devising a new diet on a full stomach, having done so a hundred times, a number far in excess of what it takes to teach wisdom to a Pavlovian dog. There was a brief rape fantasy, not so quickly brought under control, in which he discovered an attractive girl scout lost in the forest. He led the hundred and thirteen pound waif to a woodland stream where she (the usual hygiene) bathed. Then he pounced like a cat, swerving back over to his own side of the yellow line to miss a blue pickup. Certainly his first rape fantasy in memory had to be attributed to the leakage of sauerbraten into his veins. He corrected the fantasy by only putting it in a third of the way, and prolonging it into an afternoon of heartfelt bliss where it was he, Warlock, who exercised all of the good sense. The poor thing was crazy for him. She couldn't be stopped.

He checked into a modest motel on a hill outside of town, rejecting the fancier digs near the Coast Guard station as being too obvious. The food had settled to the point that he could get back on his mental toes. Hudley jumped into the middle of the large bed still gnawing furiously at a greasy veal knuckle he had secured for the dog at the restaurant. He pondered battling the dog for the knuckle but didn't feel up to the strain. A dog needs a vacation from strife. While sorting through his gear he remembered Diana saying that tonight was the summer solstice and it now occurred to him that that meant the longest day and shortest night of the year. He knew there were additional meanings but Anthropology 101 was a long time ago. Diana had so many nutty interests: on his forty-second birthday the December before, she had told him that he was lucky in terms of Chinese mythology because he was entering his seventh seven. He had made light of her statement in front of Clete and La Verne. She had huffed off for a walk in a blizzard, loving winter as she did—skating, skiing, tobogganing, walking—while he only pretended he did.

He checked the contents of a survival waist pack his father had given him years back for Christmas. Warlock had only taken it along at Clete's insistence, reminding him that they had occasionally been lost while fishing. There was a flashlight that no longer worked which meant it was no longer a flashlight; a German-made compass, a capsule of paraffin-protected matches, a Swiss army knife, a slight but large piece of material called a Space Blanket, a tin cup, some hooks and fish line, a flare, and a package of dried food and jerky he tossed in the wastebasket. No snacks today. He had brought along Diana's bird book and binoculars as a cover if he needed to sneak up on Rabun's land. He had rehearsed the vision of a group of thieving, burly woodchoppers discovering him in a thicket, at which point he would merely announce that he was an official Audubon bird watcher. No need for the retards to know how close to mayhem they were, what with the heat, the .38 invisibly packed at his shoulder.

It was easy to find the first corner of the property line some thirteen miles west of Grand Marais. You simply counted the section lines on the county map, which were a mile apart. He turned north on a two track log road, ostensibly toward Lake Superior. The road became rough going after a half mile so he parked, walking along jauntily looking for surveyor stakes beneath the ferns, the dog following with the veal knuckle still in his jaws.

Within a half hour Warlock was incomprehensibly lost. At the end of a full hour it was hopeless. Twilight had come and gone. In despair he gathered an immense pile of wood on a knoll looking down at a creek. Hudley whined and disappeared into the gathering dark.

23

Warlock looked with some satisfaction at his woodpile. A small fire burned near a bed of green ferns on which he had spread the Space Blanket. There was a tin cup of water near the fire, hopefully on the verge of boiling—he was excruciatingly thirsty but imagined a dead animal lolling in the muck upstream from where he had drawn the water. My small kingdom for a flashlight. The pistol and knife were fine but you could scarcely shoot and stab the night. He would have to wait for the enemy to pounce into the frail ring of light the fire threw. This wouldn't be a good time for Hudley to pull a surprise, no sudden playful leap out of the dark. He might just get hurt. Dad had once said when they were lost while trout fishing, "The pioneers had it a lot harder than we're having it, Son." This was before Dad had acquired the cretinoid macho lingo of the big city detective. But the trouble with the pioneers is that they largely knew what they were doing. Way back, when, in an undergrad American Studies class, a dipshit coed had asked what pioneer women used for sanitary napkins, and a bullnecked jock had shouted out "corn cobs" to a roar of approval. This was an unlikely event at Oxford, Warlock thought at the time, knowing full well that nearly all of the huge institutions of the Midwest were not so much universities as jerrybuilt vocational centers providing bumwads for the economy. In any event, his B.S. and M.B.A. were for nought in a forest where data processing machinery and charitable foundations were noticeably absent: and where man's-best-friend scooted off at nightfall. Perhaps he was trying to lead me back to the car? Unlikely at the speed he was running. It was a jungle. The dried fruit and jerky back in the motel wastebasket might have added up to an offbeat little stew. There had been a couple of those airline two-ounce bottles of whiskey in the survival kit but he had withdrawn them in a time of need. This was certainly an opportune moment to begin fasting and quit drinking. It was odd to have a wallet thick with expense money and not so much as a tea bag to comfort oneself. The imaginary girl scout walks drowsily up from the creek and spreads herself on the Space Blanket. Throw me the pork. No. Be my friend. No. Keep me warm. No. Let's run away. But we don't have a flashlight. He sank to a crouch as an owl beat overhead with the sound of sails rumpling in light wind. He applied a noxious mosquito dope to face, head, neck, hands and ankles, piled more wood on the fire and lay down on the crinkly blanket in time to hear the first chorus of yipes from coyotes. "Oh Jesus. Now I lay me down to sleep I pray the Lord my soul to keep bless all the children throughout the world who are cold, sick and hungry." Even me. Coyotes do not attack man. They're just singing. They did not really have to pick this fucking spot. Luckily it was warm and luckily Diana had offered the consolation of it being the shortest night of the year —way up here, about ten to five—seven hours. Banning any

other choices he could guts it out, by god. And come out better
for it. Oh, a night in the woods, no inconvenience, really, part
of the job, you know. He dozed, but there was an image of
Diana with a black and he was jolted awake. The black must
be me in blackface. Gather your pluck. The great Gauguin
must have slept on the South Sea beaches when forced there
by poverty, or tripped there by rum, likely with a dusky wahine.
Were there mosquitoes in Tahiti? No bears, certainly A new
cattle prod up the spine. Bears. Big bears. But they mostly
came to campsites for food and the last food hereabouts was
the veal knuckle in Hud's mouth. He's still chewing it some-
wheres, probably in the car where he didn't lead me. Diana
wanted to see a grizzly in Wyoming but no deal in the Yellow-
stone traffic jam. The coyotes seemed to come closer and he
fingered the .38, but they raced down the far side of the creek
bed and in moments he could barely hear them. Good rid-
dance. He'd only seen a dead one but this was even more scary,
he thought. Hunting with Air Force buddies in Texas. This
Mexican-Indian who was a jet mechanic said they could shoot
a javelina and barbecue it, maybe screw some Indian girls if we
bought lots of beer. It was so hot and Baxter from up in Maine
was way ahead and they heard him screaming I got one, I got
one. It wasn't a javelina but a good-sized boar and he said shit
a pig's a pig when they beat him on the back laughing. I
cleaned it with the Indian and we gave Baxter the huge balls.
What should I do with them? Get them grafted on said Klein.
The Indian's relatives were sheep ranchers and scraped all the
hair off and roasted it. Warlock slept then, thinking of Diana's
music, and imagining her face at its most demure and lovely
but it tended to change to her face at the farthest shore of
sexual passion. I sure can't control my mind. Snore. Then the

brief dream came roaring in, the antipodes of promise and grace: Mom was a trout with a woman's face flopping on a riverbank, and Dad pushed him into haunted basements, then he whirled around the sky sometimes upside down, and Diana was cutting at his leg, naked with a bunch of men behind her, the boar with its shiny, grotesque face was standing beside the fire talking to him, in basso, jolly tones but in Spanish; Diana was biting his dick and laughing. His hand was hot and he yelled. Too close to the fire. Oh my god. He yelled again— FUCK THIS PLACE. He was angry now and sipped at his tin cup of hot water and ashes. Barely after two A.M., and at least three more hours. He stomped around the fire then added more wood. Maybe he couldn't trust Diana but that was slipping back into the dream. Except for once with that photographer when they were more or less engaged. That wasn't her fault. Another distant coyote. When they were dragging the boar back to the car they stopped at a creek to wash off the dried blood. In a grove of cottonwoods Baxter yelled "Come over here." There was a big, dead coyote with a few yellow cottonwood leaves resting on him. What killed him? Old age said the Indian, look at that gray hair on his muzzle. Baxter took out his knife to take the ears for the hell of it, but the Indian said no it's bad luck so he didn't. Now he got the feeling that he could retrace his steps to the car. He stepped out of the light of the roaring fire and saw the deepest throw of stars of his life. Must be billions and the Milky Way like a waist down the middle. Jesus. Beautiful but no night for straying. Then there was a scream so penetrating that he could recapture it ever afterwards; thin and prolonged, it repeated itself twice. His hair tingled and ruffled, became damp, and his breath held until it exploded of its own accord. He was back near the fire with the gun in his hand without knowing how either of them got there. He had chosen a knoll without even a tree to back up to. He peered into the dark in the direction of the scream until his eyes were dry. Some of the wood was wet and greenish and the fire bellowed with smoke, and anyone approaching the fire might have hesitated at the sight of the man on the knoll. But no one was out there, not even a religion. He sat down cross-legged, utterly giving up. His eyes were still open but he wasn't seeing anything, not past, present, future. He had been frightened out of his wits. Jesus, Dad, and Diana disappeared. After a while he crawled back to his ferns, hearing a first bird call, however premature it might be. The fire burned low and smokeless now and he could see the stars clearly without wanting to count them. Be fun to go out there and see them close up. Wasn't he called Warlock himself, for god's sake, for thirty years? He belonged out here. If something wants to come along it will surely get its ass kicked. More birds. Moist. Dew falling. First squawk of crow. Nice to dress Diana in green leaves or green grass of the green you see in England. All the birds on the earth now started. Where had they been all night? Then a streak of light in the east and a little breeze off the lake.

24

In the bleary daylight, across the dead fire, there were feet and, higher, green legs that even higher were attached to a man.

"Good morning," the young man said.

"Good morning." Warlock rolled off the ferns and onto his feet.

"I have to assume you had a fire permit?" There was a Forest Service insignia on the man's shirt.

"Fuck off, junior." Warlock strode down the hill toward the creek to wash up, with the man trotting along behind.

"I'm sorry but I'll have to write a citation. . . ." The man interrupted himself when Warlock took off his safari jacket. The .38 gleamed from the shoulder holster in the morning sun.

"So write. You'll have to go to Washington to check me out. Then you'll be back planting trees with the kids. What screams in the night around here?"

"Pardon, sir. I didn't hear anything."

"Last night. I heard three screams."

"Has to be a bobcat or owl taking a rabbit. Rabbits scream. It sounds like a girl."

"Sure does, kiddo." Warlock felt much refreshed from the cold creek water. He lit a cigarette and took out his wallet, handing two C-notes to the young man. "I got a few hours work for you."

"I can't take money," the man protested, letting the bills drop to the ground.

"Then leave it there. Two things. Is this water good to drink and where the fuck is my car?"

"The creek comes from a spring up that hill. It's fine. Your car is only about a quarter a mile to the south. There's an angry dog in it chewing on something."

Warlock knelt down and drank until his teeth ached. When he got up he noted that the bills were no longer on the grass. The plight of the civil servant.

It took most of the day to cover Rabun's two thousand acres by Forest Service Jeep. The young man, Bob by name, was first-rate at the maps, freeing Warlock to take notes. The thievery was cautious and selective, invisible from the more traveled log roads. Near the end of the tour they had added up some one hundred and eighty illegally cut acres.

"I can't appear in court on this," Bob said with extreme nervousness.

"We don't need you, so relax."

"It's just that I live up here and got a wife and kids."

"Everybody does. Kids like chickenshit, Dagwood daddies."

"I resent that."

"Go ahead . . ." Warlock suddenly held up his hand and the Jeep rumbled to a stop. He heard a chainsaw off to the right down a long gulley. He put on his binoculars and eased out of the vehicle.

"You'll get your ass kicked," Bob hissed.

Warlock moved quietly off through the forest toward the chainsaw noise. He quickly came upon a well hidden blue Ford pickup. Was it the same pickup that had swerved at him during his sex fantasy near Epoufette the day before? Not likely. As a precaution he took the .33 rifle off the rack and pitched it out into the ferns. Then, as an afterthought, he pulled a valve core on a back tire.

They were at the edge of a clearing trimming a giant hemlock that they had just felled, making his heart jump wildly. He walked directly into the clearing, then stared through the binoculars at the top of a tree above the two woodchoppers, drawing the binoculars down through the tree until he had them in focus. Big fuckers. They stared back in amazement, then walked toward Warlock so that he had to keep readjusting the focus. They paused at a range that they were able to see his pistol. He dropped the binoculars to his chest.

"Whadda you think you're doing? This is private property." The voice was not without edge.

"No shit, Sherlock. I'm on an Audubon bird count. I got permission."

"What kind of birds?" the other said, obviously the dumber of the two.

"Cooper's hawk and Connecticut warbler." He had done his homework.

"This ain't Connecticut, so get on out of here."

"Sorry, I must have taken the wrong turn." They oddly sounded as if they were from Kentucky, Warlock thought. Probably outside talent.

"I said get on out of here." The larger of the two was now probing for weakness.

"Say it again and I'll blow your guts all over the clearing. Fox food, you know. Go back to cutting limbs."

"Fuck you," they said in unison but went back to cutting limbs.

Bob drove him back to the Subaru and he added an extra hundred bonus, saying good-bye. Hudley had nearly finished the veal knuckle and pretended that nothing had been amiss in the past twenty-four hours. He was covered with flies and snapped at them with vicious clacks, protecting the remnant of his knuckle.

Back at the motel Warlock checked by phone with different companies on the worth of Bob's estimates of the total board feet of white pine, hemlock, oak and maple that had been stolen. He totaled up the figures then took a shower. He would wait until tomorrow morning to call Rabun, not wanting him to know how fast and easy it had been. He lay back on the bed for a quick snooze, shoving Hudley off with a heel, but somehow didn't feel tired. Or hungry, for that matter, which was even more surprising. He must eat or, in the long range, he would disappear. Simple as that. It was action itself that removed temporarily his need for sleep or food. All that fresh air and movement. He decided that life itself was like bad art, and action peeled off the lattice, fretwork, filagree; in short, the drivel. He discontinued, for the time being, this train of thought when it led to rape, fistfights, murder and war. Some fine lines must be drawn. Hudley tore apart his bag of kibble but Warlock couldn't stop his eyes from closing. A mosquito bite on his dick woke him at twilight. His stomach growled unbearably and he dressed at top speed, imagining a meal that reason told him wouldn't be available locally. In a stroke of caution he hid the Rabun timber papers in the back of the television set. He grabbed Diana's copy of Roger Tory Peterson for want of anything else to read at dinner. From lack of habit he nearly forgot the .38, but strapped it on to revive his diminishing sense of mystery. The shifting faces of reality, he thought, driving to the only bona fide restaurant in the village; it had been closed a full half hour but he could still see the lucky piggies in there eating. How unfair. An old gent in madras shorts and yellow knee socks told him there were steaks at the bar downtown. Hudley jumped out the car window, growled at the old man and took a dump on the sidewalk.

"I'm sorry. Jeez, Hudley, you jerk."

"Maybe my wife will slip in that shit and break her neck. Then I can go to Florida alone. Here's hoping." The old man stared off at the last light, sunken deeply in his reverie.

Warlock ate a rib steak looking at bird pictures, then a sirloin with home fries when the chancre of hunger still seemed unassuaged. Diana was quite the birdwatcher. It seemed impossible that there were so many different kinds. Had god been indecisive? Why both crow and raven, for instance?

"There's Mr. Birdy-fucker." The two burly woodchoppers were at the bar with a dapper-looking, older woodsman wearing the same expensive wool shirt as Warlock. Must be the mastermind criminal. He approached tentatively.

"My boys said that you stole their rifle and let the air out of their tire," the man said with a smile.

"If I look like I'd steal a rifle, so do you. They felled a hemlock that had been a nesting sight for a pileated woodpecker."

"I see," the mastermind said, trying to estimate the gravity of the situation.

"You might be interested in my life list." Warlock pushed the Peterson across the table. "I'm up to three hundred and twenty-three. I'm going to Hawaii at Christmas to pick up thirty more. Tell those jerkoffs at the bar not to bother me. I got twenty years of karate and I love to turn dummies into hamburger."

25

Needless to say, he hightailed it out of town. It was easy enough to talk rough in daylight when you had the drop on someone, but night changed the odds. He barreled down Route 77 toward Seney, "barreled" being a flattering term for what the four cylinder Subaru would do on a straightaway. It was doubtless time to buy a muscle car, not something obvious like a Porsche; the job seemed to demand a black Trans Am. It was difficult to drive fast with one eye on the rearview mirror and a Trans Am, so he had read, would outrun anything.

The panic of the departure only slowly subsided. Hudley had dashed around the room barking, which hadn't helped. Then in a nervous gesture he had discovered that he had neglected to load the pistol. My god. Few of the fans of the movie *Deliverance* realized that the Great North owned backwoods feebs who far exceeded in threat their southern counterparts. Every little town had a bully named Tiny who would eat fifteen hamburgers or five fried chickens, drink a case of beer and beat up on some hapless stranger. The recent surge of marijuana into the outback had helped calm these thugs: now, some ten years out of date, they were wont to wear their hair long and exchange greetings such as "Peace, baby," or *"¿Qué pasa?"*

Warlock felt safe enough by Newberry to stop at a party store and buy a pint of schnapps to tamp down the steaks which were acting up. Fear was bad for digestion. A fear diet would be big on rice and poached fish. Soda crackers and soup. Nothing heavy. The schnapps immediately did its yeoman's service and he decided to spend the night in Sault Ste. Marie. Rabun would probably want to send up a lawyer right away and Warlock could arrange to drop the papers at the airport. He turned the radio dial with irritation: there was an enervating controversy in country music about who was, and who wasn't, a "real" cowboy. The real ones he had seen in Texas and Wyoming appeared to be an impoverished, unenviable lot. Early in his teens he had asked Dad for a pair of cowboy boots and Dad had confided that cowboys "fucked sheep." This information tended to color his views of the West. Now on the dark highway to Sault Ste. Marie it occurred to him that he had been gullible. He took a deep swig of schnapps, almost in anger. Dad had no doubt fibbed to save himself the price of the boots! If you weren't wary your entire view of reality could become discolored. The sudden notion that reality could be scrubbed utterly clean of lies and illusions was discomfiting. You might not like it that way, he thought. In high school his friend Dick was always claiming that his mother didn't love him. Warlock took the bull by the horns and one day after football practice, over milk and cookies, he confronted the woman. Dick fled the kitchen. "No, I don't love him. He's a dreadful little nose-picking shit. He was big at birth and ruined my body. I could have been an actress. I hate him." She finally ran off downstate with a Chrysler salesman, who was later brought to justice for swiping a DeSoto out of the used car lot.

Sault Ste. Marie proved a grand morale boost. You could sense the clean winds of Canada sweeping across St. Mary's River. The motel clerk, an older lady reading *Christian Century*, had peered into the dark at the barking Hudley. Why hadn't he parked down the street?

"We can't accept dogs. I'm sorry."

"Please give this to the church of your choice," said Warlock, noticing her magazine and slipping a hundred on top of the room payment. "I'm very tired."

"Why thank you. I guess dogs are god's creatures, too."

"They sure are. Jesus was partial to little lambs. Of course I'm not bringing in a lamb."

"Of course not."

"Of course not."

The closest bar turned out to be a student dive and he almost turned around, loathing students, when he caught the eye of a dark haired maiden. Maybe one drink, he thought. The music was loud and terrible, mixing as it did with a half dozen pinball machines at the back of the bar. The drink was so weak that he ordered another shot put in with no little contempt. He went for broke with a long, somber, heartfelt stare. She sure was pretty as a speckled pup. She fell to the bait and left her group of sallow youth.

"Why are you staring at me?"

"Does a cat got an ass? You're lovely." He tried to bite off the inappropriate question but it was too late. She seemed amused, looking him up and down and baring white teeth with a smile.

"My name is Aurora. I'm a Chippewa Indian."

"I'm Johnny. I'm just a white guy."

"Don't make fun of me." She sat on the stool next to him and swiveled daffily.

"I'm not making fun of you. Believe me, I know your plight better than most." She was a prime piece and he didn't want to blow it. His brain strained wildly for information about Indians. At Diana's insistence he had hastily read *Cheyenne Autumn.* The only other book was Oliver La Farge's *Laughing Boy;* but that was years back.

"Let's not talk about my people. Let's talk about us." She ran a finger suggestively between his own.

"Right. We're all high and dry. Why dwell on the past?" Off the Indian hook. He stared as she raised a knee, draped by a light summer skirt, against the bar. The skirt slipped down and there, plain as day, was a thigh that rumbled his wiener.

"You're not like these others. They know nothing." She gestured at the students.

"I guess I've been around."

"This place is too noisy to talk. Are you a rich white man? On the reservation none of us are rich. It is very cold in the winter."

"You might say I'm well heeled." He hadn't expected this pro shot—probably short on rent. Rabun owed him one for hazard duty.

On the way out he thought he heard her murmur something to the effect that "May your dick grow as big as your heart" but knew this sort of irony was improbable up in the sticks. Unfortunately, on the way back to the motel she insisted on stopping for a takeout pizza, with everything. Pizza was perhaps his least favorite food, he thought, hoping it wasn't a bad omen. Rather than stand there in the nasty smelling glare of the parlor he slipped next door for a six-pack and pile of magazines.

Back at the motel the introduction to Hudley was difficult. Warlock assumed that Indians were new to the dog, but Aurora deftly won him over with niblets of pepperoni. Then an entire piece of the pizza when it had cooled sufficiently. She ate quickly and enormously but had been kind enough to strip down to her undies. He drank a largish glass of whiskey from his travel bottle, feeling the trepidation of approaching a new species. He was amazed that so slight a girl, he guessed about a hundred pounds, could wolf down that much pizza with three beers, yet her tan tummy showed no bulge. They must work her hard on the reservation. He envisioned her scrubbing her buckskin clothes by a river while being watched by deer and raccoons. There was a minuscule gobbet of tomato sauce on her neck embedded with a speck of oregano, a red jewel of sorts. He reached for her.

"Not so fast. My stomach was hungry for food. Now I need a shower."

"I'll take one with you. We'll pretend it's a waterfall."

"Why?" She looked a little alarmed as he speedily undressed, wanting to encourage hygiene.

"I saw this painting of an Indian maiden under a waterfall. It wasn't dirty. There were these raccoons and deer watching."

"Far out. Many times have I stood under a waterfall."

She was almost too much of a spitfire, and at times during the next hour he wondered if he had bit off more than he could chew. She had a nervous disposition, orgasm resistant, or hard to bring off, as the magazines say. His jaw ached to the point that he imagined a few days of Rabun's porridge diet. You can't say I'm insensitive to her wants, he thought. These Indian girls knew positions that Warlock thought modern but must be a tribal legacy.

He awoke earlier than he had hoped to find her weeping and fully dressed, standing beside the bed. She was shaking the hundred dollar bill he had stuffed in her wallet. She said she wasn't a whore. She said she wasn't an Indian. She was of Armenian descent from Detroit, a third grade teacher taking a summer course at Lake Superior State College. She kept the money.

"Meet me at the bar for lunch?" He had checked her wallet in the middle of the night when he got up to pee and knew the whole story. The slamming door inferred a negative.

26

At mid-morning in the motel a psychiatrist, had one been handy, would have diagnosed the first anxiety attack of War-lock's life. It began with the usual sense of displacement, the eternal question of "what am I doing here?" The spark for the displacement was a liquor advertisement in a magazine, quoting Robert Service's "The Men That Don't Fit In":

> There's a race of men that don't fit in,
> A race that can't stay still;
> So they break the hearts of kith and kin,
> And they roam the world at will.

Service was Dad's favorite poet, he remembered. The graphics in the ad featured a man in fur hat and full length fur coat staring off across a roaring fire and frozen lake in the wilder-ness. Very impressive, in a way. There was an invisible sense of a dozen tethered malamutes in the background. Warlock deeply identified with the picture which was a glyph of Cain, or Ishmael, at full roam; doomed, haunted, but not boring. He had been trying to write a witty rehearsal for his belated phone call to Rabun, became exacerbated, and looked at the magazine. There was a lump in his throat that spread into dizziness, as if earth had increased the speed of its rotations. The panic increased and his breath was short with the ensuing vacuum of hyperventilation. The four walls billowed. He was homesick for Diana, the ritual of the *Free Press*, hours of thought, shopping and cooking dinner, watching Walter Cronkite, educational TV with rococo music, lovemaking, his own bed with its special pillow from his youth. A tear fell, then another. He was a child again with big hands, big head and big feet, but with no body. The anxiety waxed and waned for an hour, and was akin to waking and discovering you had twenty-two fingers. There were simply no options. He had been bound into a system more tightly constructed than Marx's view of the working class. It took only a few minutes to flit like a chickadee through the entirety of his life. Did it only come down to this two hundred pounder weeping on a motel bed, consoling a dog that was worried about the master's behavior? Did Diana really love him? His previously sublimated antennae made him know that a woman can only love weakness until she becomes bored with mothering it. Then she looks elsewhere out of superior sanity. Marilyn hadn't wanted children and now she had two in Pasadena, California. Diana didn't want children "just yet"— thinking that she might yet resolve her thwarted ambition to be a doctor. Had Marilyn and Diana, with female intuition, seen him as a bad bet on the future? Doubtless. Was the long repressed idea of Gauguin grabbing for his heart and mind? Doubtless. Had the pressure of a failed life increased exponentially to the point that it created that dream of the future? Doubtless. He knew it. Despite his disingenuousness he was no dummy. He was suffering a war of ghosts. Was that firelit Webelos ceremony, when he was twelve and became Warlock, preying on him now? Doubtless. Was it only a lame superstition, a toady bow to the darkness that surrounds us? Yes and no. Civilization certainly hadn't panned out. Warlock frankly knew from the revived memory of a college mythology course that he was at the awesome crossroads where the hero must continue the quest or turn his back on it. Many are called, but few are chosen, the Bible said. Deep in the night the wandering hero peeks in the winter frosted window and sees the happy bourgeoisie at a laden table before a happy hearth. He turns away, with care sitting on his faded cheek. . . . There was a knock on the door. It was the Christian lady motel clerk.

"Mr. Lundgren?"

"Yes," he croaked, his strong hands around Hudley's throat, choking off a bark.

"It's past check-out time. Will you be staying?"

"Chalk me up for another night, ma'am."

"The guild ladies wanted me to thank you for the donation. We're aiding the Indians out on the reservation."

"Wonderful." The struggle with Hudley was getting out of hand. He resolved not to lose the petty battle. He took the remaining piece of cold pizza off the dresser and shoved it in the dog's mouth.

"There was a crying Indian girl making a phone call in the office this morning. I hope there wasn't any trouble?"

"No trouble. Her mother died. It was a sad occasion."

"That's terrible . . ." she began, but he let Hudley go. The old cunt was driving him witless. The dog hit the door with a roar and a smash. There was a shriek. The gesture would certainly cost Rabun another hundred bucks. Now for the gloomy phone.

"Rabun. This is Warlock."

"War what?"

"Lock. A code name. It's Johnny."

"Oh. In the U.P.?"

"Yes. I busted the timber thieving ring. Send a lawyer up tomorrow to Sault Ste. Marie. I'll leave the papers at the Hertz desk. He can take them to the state police and prosecutor."

"Tomorrow is the Friday before the Fourth."

"Use your weight. Christ, man, a forester made a conservative estimate of your loss at a hundred fifty grand, mostly prime hardwood. I caught them red handed. It got a little rough."

"Oh my god. Are you okay? I didn't think you were that smart."

"Fine. I am that smart. This is just a beginning."

Warlock left a message at the hospital telling Diana he would be home by Saturday evening. He needed rest and his vision of rest included another night with a certain Armenian Indian by the name of Aurora. He got her number with some difficulty from the college. She was asleep and very cross.

"This is Johnny. . . ."

"I don't want to talk to you," she interrupted. "Good-bye."

"Just a minute. I thought we'd go for a drive and a swim. Have a gourmet dinner and champagne."

"I'm a vegetarian and I have to study."

"You ate pepperoni last night."

"No I didn't. I fed it to your macho dog."

"Some of the pepperoni juice no doubt leaked into the cheese. You're tainted."

"Not funny. Now I'm . . ."

"I knew you were a vegetarian." He knew he was losing her. It was time to be inventive.

"How come?"

"You tasted so good. Ladies that are meat eaters don't taste nearly as good."

"Far out. It's weird but I've been told that before."

"I just busted a big case and I wanted to celebrate. I made a bundle. Don't worry, I'm not a cop. Sort of a cross between a private dick and a spy." He was moving along now, attracting her self-interest, greed, adding a dollop of mystery.

"Geez, I don't know. What time?"

"About ten minutes or sooner. I got a hardon. I'll try to save it for you."

"Johnny, you're crazy!" He loved her merry peal of laughter.

While he waited he read some nasty letters in *Penthouse* to further goad his lust. Reality was amazing: one minute he was having a nervous breakdown, and the next moment he broke through the soup of despondency with a clean hammerlock on the future. Had that sacred summer solstice night in the forest imbued him with new powers, he wondered? It was possible. The slump only fueled the reaffirmation. He quickly passed over a series of enema letters. Warlock had never understood how anyone could think that peepee and caca were sexy.

It was just short of a half hour before Aurora's knock. He welcomed her with his dingo wobbling out the front of his terry cloth robe. She dove on it with a wonderful shriek of laughter. The dog growled and he scored a direct disciplinary hit with Diana's bird book. He eased her panties off and drove his head up under her skirt. Some are brownish and some are pinkish. *Pourquoi?*

27

A day passed. A night passed. Then another day and another night. Saturday dawned as the lovers slept. Saturday after Saturn, that vast globy iceberg in the heavens. A day of saturnalia for many a wage earner but not for Warlock who, frankly, was fucked out. If you were the unattractive ceiling fixture in the motel room you would see him strung out precariously along the edge of the mattress as if trying to escape her within the boundaries of sleep; this quasi-Indian, this hyperthyroid vixen, this crazed schoolmarm from Melvindale, a suburb of Detroit, named oddly after a pioneer who went by the handle of Marvin.

It hadn't been all beer and skittles. Rabun had partially broken cover by giving the lawyer from Detroit the motel phone number.

"Feingold here, Rabun's lawyer. I just Leared up from Metro. I'm over with the state police now. Good work. Get over to the post. The Luce County prosecutor's on his way."

"No." At the time Warlock had been preoccupied with a trinket Aurora had selected from the many at a porn store.

"No, what?"

"I'm under orders not to break cover. You have all the information you need."

"Don't be absurd. What's that buzzing sound?"

"I'm at a barber shop. Hear?" He withdrew the trinket and held it to the phone for an unnecessary length of time. "Did you hear it?"

"Are you crazy?"

"Don't fuck with me, Charley. I've done my job. Do yours. I'd hate to see you back on a paper route. Get it?"

"I see. But you'll eventually have to testify. . . ."

"Great. I'll wear a Donald Duck mask." He hung up with a smash.

"You must be a big deal?" Aurora asked, her eyes still glazed by the trinket.

"Yes and no. No one really knows who I am."

"Not even your wife?"

"My wife?"

"I went through your wallet."

"She knows nothing. It's a lonely, evil job. You play the hunches. Sometimes you live. Sometimes you die."

"Oh my god, darling."

"It's okay. I haven't died yet."

The affair had ended on a bittersweet note. He had maintained the enigmatic charade on the phone with detectives, the lawyers, the prosecutor. They were all initially irritated, but then grew to enjoy the mystery of it. But Warlock was fatigued at answering the same or similar questions dozens of times. He and Aurora took a drive to a little lake in the forest where she and her school chums went to drink and smoke dope. Hudley had created the first cloud of the afternoon by jumping in the lake with a roar, and swimming out toward two fishermen in a canoe.

"What do we do?" they hollered from out in the lake.

"Hit him with your paddles." They flailed at the dog until he turned around. He sat on the shore quietly, then, as if waiting for vengeance.

"Why don't you ever see Armenia on a map?" he had asked innocently.

"Greece and Turkey gobbled up the country of my fathers."

"Hungary fried Turkey in Greece. Remember that one?"

"It's not funny, Johnny."

"I didn't present it as a world class joke."

"What do you know of our tragedy, you bastard?"

"I didn't wipe out your fucking country. Ease up."

Later, at dinner at a place called the Antlers, things got even rougher. His fork and knife had been poised over a massive porterhouse as she picked at a salad and radishes.

"How can you put that in your mouth? Yuk."

"I cut it in inch squares with knife and fork. Watch." Pretty good, but Dad is right. They just don't hang meat long enough anymore.

"Watching you makes me want to puke."

"Keep it up and you're going to be eating some of it." He tamped a driblet of blood off his lip with his napkin. One of his least favorite things was negativism during his dinner.

"You wouldn't dare," she hissed, her anger no doubt fed by bad diet. He could almost feel the grating of those endless bags of corn chips she ate in bed.

"You'll never know when it's coming. . . ." He interrupted himself to stare at the ceiling in convulsed horror. She looked up in alarm, with her mouth popping open, as mouths always do. She got an especially bloody square from near the bone.

"You motherfucker," she screamed spitting the meat nearly the length of a good broad-jump. She ran toward the restroom sobbing.

Warlock noted that their little scene was a show stopper. It had been prime time Friday evening in the best restaurant in town and all the eaters in the house, some swiveling uncomfortably from their booths, were staring at him. He took a largish bit of meat, wondering if a vindication was in order. He spoke firmly and loudly as he chewed.

"I guess I owe you all an apology. You're paying good hard-earned dollars for an evening out on the town, and what you've been through, candidly, is a mud bath. That was my little sister, more precious to me than life itself. Don't take her curse seriously. It's idiomatic of course. I never had a thought about Mom who died when we were kids. Anyway, to make a long story short, I drove five hundred miles from Akron, Ohio, today because Sis is a college student with a drug problem. I'm a doctor and it's my professional opinion that she will need years of hospitalization. . . ." The manager approached, nervously testing the air for the right move. "So I'm very sorry. As a gesture of apology I want to buy the drink of your choice for everyone in the house." The manager led the applause. Warlock felt sweat trickling down his chest. Several people came over to shake his hand, including an older couple who assured him that their prayers would follow. A waitress whispered shyly that Aurora was out in the car waiting for him. He dropped two more of his dwindling supply of C-notes on the table, shook hands with the manager and left.

It was perhaps a coincidence that she extracted the price of a gram of coke before she would forgive him. He waited in the

Subaru outside a student bar while she made the purchase, petting the somber Hudley who was still thinking of the fishermen with paddles. What if they got busted? What would the police do with his not exactly beloved dog?

Back in the room she went through the ritual of chopping the drug into little white lines. He had witnessed this nonsense before, though he had never partaken of the drug. Warlock's friend, Garth, the avant-garde artist, merely poured it in a spoon and snorted away.

"How can you put that up your nose? It makes me puke."

She looked at the ceiling in horror. His eyes followed hers as she flicked a large pinch in his mouth. He pretended he was chewing a chunk of steak, then went through a mock Jekyll-Hyde change of character. By dawn at 5 A.M. they were out of coke, whiskey, schnapps, corn chips, and were smoking Aurora's last joint. He felt sad and depraved.

"Johnny, I'm no good at good-byes. Just tell me we'll meet again someday."

"We'll meet again someday."

"Say it better than that."

"Someday, somewhere, we'll meet again." He felt a strange urge to sing a show tune, but could remember only bits. She began to snore, ever so delicately. *"Love me or leave me. Let me be lonely."*

28

The drive home was long and mournful. A mere three hours of sleep left a hole in creation when a body normally required ten hours. Always the enumerator, he made his ninth unsuccessful phone call in five days to Diana at a roadside booth. He needed deeply to whine to Diana. Where was she? Was someone tupping his heifer? Impossible. The miles became endless and he stomped on the gas. The shoulder holster itched in the July heat and he seriously considered pitching the .38 as he crossed the Mackinac Bridge. Warlock simply wasn't a gun person. He would clean the pistol and put it permanently back in the closet like a retired gunslinger. "I will hone my body into fine steel," he said aloud. Maybe buy a bulletproof vest or brass knuckles. He would work silently and guns made a lot of noise, though they don't sound like the siren immediately behind him. Hudley jumped furiously around the car barking at the squad car tailgating the Subaru. He discovered that somehow in his dank reverie he had worked the car up to seventy-five. Shit. He stopped and rolled up the windows to avoid dog problems. The officer was walking up when he remembered the pistol. He got out slowly. Dad always said that fast movements tended to put cops on edge.

"I'm sorry. I guess I was lost in thought and going too fast." He handed over his license and registration.

"Seventy-five." They stared at each other, both wearing reflector sunglasses; both knights of the surrealist age, Warlock thought. The cop went back to the squad car for a radio check. Warlock moved away from the Subaru to avoid the barking. He looked off at the vast Pigeon River Forest, only lately handed over in the usual oil industry sucker punch, according to Diana. Her ERA efforts had not exhausted her interests in nature. She was a dynamo, he thought proudly. What could she have made for dinner? Maybe to celebrate his coming home she would put on her green satin dress and garter belt with no panties. The cop's voice startled him; he had forgotten the occasion for a moment.

"Sorry to bother you, Lundgren. You must be quite a guy."

"I don't get it." He expected a ticket for going twenty miles over the limit.

"Well, the lawyer gave our boys the motel number and we ran a check on you. We had to. Anyway, congratulations."

"Thank you. I should have been more careful."

"It's not my business but you should be careful about that girl. She's a known drug user."

"Oh my god!" Warlock faked recoil, shaking his head. "You just never know these days. She said she was a schoolteacher."

"Just a tip. Don't worry. We won't blow your cover. Bye. Hang loose."

"Hang loose." He waved as the trooper laid a stretch of rubber and smoke. He was not normally paranoid but now felt queasy at his foolishness. It was probably only professional courtesy that had kept them from making a dope raid on his motel. Think of the shame Diana and Dad would have felt. How would Hudley have gotten back home? A dark temptress had almost got his ass in a sling. From now on no dope and adultery, plus he would only use pay phones.

By the time he reached Traverse City he had regained much of his composure by using a nostrum Diana had tried to teach him. During a particularly depressing part of the winter he had taken to sitting at the kitchen table for hours at a time "just thinking." One night she sneaked up behind him.

"Leave yourself alone," she screamed.

He had fallen off the chair as if protecting himself from a fatal blow. "You do that again and I'll kick your ass," he blubbered, his heart still at full flutter.

"I'm trying to help you, Johnny. You're becoming paralyzed."

"I might have died of a heart attack for Christ's sake."

"You didn't. It was worth the risk. You're going mad from self-pity, self-concern, self-indulgence. You begin every fucking sentence with 'I' or 'my.' You say 'I'm hungry,' 'My stomach is upset,' 'I'm horny,' 'My heart is broken,' 'I hate *Kojak*,' 'I hate hamburgers,' 'I hate *Star Wars*.' 'I,I,I,I,I,I,' " she sang as if she were a mariachi singer in a Mexican cantina, then marched up to her secret room.

He had brooded for a while on the best tack against this insult. He recognized her shot as being basically true, but there was a dim-witted masculine urge to get the upper hand somehow.

"Is this some more of your Oriental bullshit?" he hollered up the stairwell. "It's fucking slant balderdash, you bitch. Why don't you move to fucking Tokyo you fucking Tokyo Rose bitch traitor." It didn't help. She turned up one of her favorite records, Stravinsky's *Petrouchka,* very loud to drown out his voice. He fought back with a B.B. King record at top volume but his head ached. Then he had gone to the bar.

Oddly, he felt, some nine months later, that her silly lesson had worked. He wouldn't admit it aloud. Dad would faint if he became a sucker for a bunch of Tojo propaganda. But in the past month since his dream of the future, Dad had somehow become less of a moving force in his life. So when he hit the Traverse City limits he yelled "Leave yourself alone," felt immediately better and stopped at a bar noted for its burgers and stuffed animal mounts. He ate the burger—after all, Diana might have neglected his dinner—directly under a very dusty great white owl. Diana certainly was shrewd. He chuckled, remembering that the day after the quarrel he had dragged one of the landlord's cherry-picking ladders out of the barn, and through the snowdrifts to the back of the house. He had climbed the ladder with some excitement, scraped the frost off the window with his fingernails and peeked in: it was disappointingly plain, featuring a black mat and cushion, a hot plate and teapot, a record player, bare white walls, a small fat figurine that faced away from the window. Did his wife worship strange gods? Maybe he was lucky—the wife of a friend in Lansing had become an obnoxious Jesus freak after Bob Dylan turned the corner.

Warlock reached home in the twilight, thrilled by a gorgeous sunset and the hills rolling down to the lake, covered by precise rows of laden cherry trees. He despised the flavor of the fruit but you sure couldn't knock the prosperity of the local farmers. It wasn't their fault that he had, at age ten, eaten a whole jar of maraschino cherries on a quarter bet. Not only had he puked a lot but the buddy never had the quarter in the first place.

She found him asleep on the couch after midnight, her note resting on his stomach, and the pistol grip glaring from its holster. Her note advising that she had a long emergency period in surgery because of an auto accident had depressed him. She was very somber after these emergency sessions and that meant the green gown and garter belt were definitely out. There was an ugly sense of embarrassment when he reflected that there had probably been a terrible accident and here he was thinking about his dick. She kissed him awake.

"Was it bad?" he murmured.

"The worst. A bunch of migrant workers in a pickup. Kids in the back. It was awful." She looked pale and exhausted. He hugged her then got up to make her a Margarita. She usually drank two, then took a five or ten milligram Valium, after these occasions.

"I'm sorry," he called from the kitchen but she had followed him.

"Johnny, please take off that gun. It scares me. Doctor Rabun said there was trouble and you made a lot of money."

"It's okay, kiddo."

"Don't give me that tough guy bullshit. I've seen gunshot wounds."

"Anything you say, baby." He took off the holster and tossed the whole works into the corner wastebasket. He handed her a drink and they clicked glasses. "You're all wound up, love, you want to play strip poker?"

"Oh god, why not." She laughed. "It beats solitaire."

29

July turned into August, August into September, September
into golden October, October into dreary November: the ancient cycle of the season was not to be denied by those sorry
fools who hated bad weather but were too poor to move south.
The books of Sigurd Olson were helping Warlock to accept the
climatic injustice of the earth with equanimity. Why piss and
moan about the weather when it's such a big part of reality,
he thought. He was toughening his spirit and body in so many
ways that he was frequently dizzy with activity. He had cleaned
and clumsily partitioned a room in the basement for his own
secret place. He had always been a little fearful of basements
but now a dark secretive basement seemed particularly suited
to his work. He had placed a massive combination lock (33-
33-33-1) on the door and was modestly irritated when Diana
had evinced no curiosity, but then her own life, too, was a
frenzy of activity: with the approaching elections her ERA
work was coming to a head.

The newfound prosperity was a boon in that it enabled him
to indulge in equipment: the secret room held new cross-

country skis waiting for snow, a graphite tennis racquet waiting for an impulse, a professional heavy punching bag and gloves, a stationary exercise bicycle, a gimmick called Bullworker, Bobby Hinds Lifeline Gym—an isokinetic rubber gimmick, a hatha-yoga book, two dumbells, and so on. And Warlock was not neglecting his mind: there were stacks of books on birds, flowers, trees, the ocean, the weather, and even a few on that perennial favorite, sex. His body was not yet as finely honed as steel but a succession of nasty diets from the Scarsdale to Craig Claiborne's low sodium masterpiece had chipped off thirteen pounds and brought him down to one eighty-seven. And not that there weren't hitches to the struggle for all around health; one day at the IGA he had spotted a cask of salt herring and hunger had flared wildly like a California brush fire. Back home he put these lovely, if ugly, fish in a big bowl of water to leech as Mom had done, then prepared in another bowl the onions, vinegar and pickling spices. The whole works were secreted in the basement room, and he counted off the forty-eight hours it took for the dish to reach maturity. He had mistakenly asked Diana to monitor his diet and she had done so with an especially inquisitive eye.

"Your breath smells like pickles and vinegar. You know pickles are sodium rich, strictly taboo. 'Fess up."

"I haven't eaten a pickle in months." He had forgotten to brush his teeth after a later afternoon herring gorge.

"Johnny, do you have pickles hidden in your room?"

"Scout's honor, no. It must be ketosis. The breath of starving people becomes foul. I read about it. India is chock full of bad breath."

"You're making such progress. I hate to see you backslide." Diana had wondered aloud at the new sexual athleticism his shaping up program had caused.

"I'll swear on a Bible that I haven't eaten a pickle. Get the Bible."

"We don't have a Bible. You know that."

"Every home should have a Bible."

"Of course, darling. I'll swipe one out of a hospital room."

His lame departure from the topic convinced her of a coverup. She easily imagined a shelf of delicacies in his room, though his admittedly strenuous workouts were audible through the heat registers.

The minute she left for work the next morning he destroyed the evidence, throwing away the last, somehow symbolic, piece of herring, though eating a bunch of the remaining pickled onions didn't seem central to the issue.

There had been a disturbing double victory dinner at Rabun's. The evening had nearly caused an anxiety attack though there had been a certain amount of forewarning. Diana was a local candidate, and among the remaining half dozen nominees, for a full scholarship for four years of medical school. The scholarship was intended to encourage talented nurses. The other occasion for celebration was the payment of Warlock's commission on the initial restitution the crooked lumberman was making in an attempt to stay out of Jackson Prison. What was there to celebrate? he wondered, as Diana and Rabun chatted about what medical school would be best suited for her. Number one in his mind was the suspense of waiting three months to see if she won. He had always wanted to know the endings of movies before he went. And what was he going to do with the seven grand cash to add to the canister of wages in the basement? Tax avoidance was a two-edged sword. And there was another upsetting factor: Rabun somehow knew about his diet and had presented an elaborate cuisine minceur dinner: a seviche of scallops, a dainty asparagus mousse, a single braised, boned quail on a bed of watercress, a dessert of red currant sherbet. All the dishes were faultless but the lack of volume after so much anticipation was utterly cruel. A single bottle of Montrachet, which Rabun appeared to hog, was also unfair; their conversation had now elapsed into the intricacies of surgical equipment, leaving him to tweedle his hungry thumbs. Anger rose slowly from deep in his empty craw.

"If I don't get a great big brandy I'm going to faint." He forced a smile as they turned to him, mildly alarmed.

"Why, of course. Please forgive me. I thought your counting calories precluded booze." Rabun hopped to a sideboard. He set a full bottle and snifter in front of Warlock.

Later, on the way home, Warlock had offered everything from amok biorhythms to low blood sugar as an excuse for his behavior. There was absolutely no question that the paltry meal had been an ineffective cushion for the amount of brandy that had landed on it. He had gone on a longish walk with Rabun's two guard dogs to clear his head and to avoid further shooting off his mouth. The brutes pranced along merrily beside him until a dim memory arose; he lit a match to check his watch —five minutes short of eleven o'clock when the dogs would become killers. All his recent running and jogging saved him as he burst toward the house in a 440-yard dash. Diana and Rabun jumped up when he came through the door.

"Dogs. Eleven. I forgot," he wheezed.

"For god's sake, man, I put the alarm on manual when I have guests."

"What if you forgot?" Fear was being displaced by embarrassment.

"I never forget. It's too important."

"I'd prefer it if my life didn't depend on someone's memory. Maybe you have hardening of the arteries and certain little memory cells aren't receiving enough blood. . . ."

"Johnny, for god's sake shut up. You're drunk and making a fool of yourself." Diana came to his side and helped him to his feet.

"He's not being a fool," Rabun kindly interjected. "In his job it's foolish to trust anyone."

"That's a terrible way to live. He shouldn't have the job," Diana hissed.

"Hold on. Hold on." Warlock raised his hands in a strong papal gesture. "With the training I'm putting myself through I could easily kill one of the beasts with my hands. In another month of hard work two won't be out of the question." He slashed the air with some dread aikido moves he had gotten out of a manual. "Why should a two hundred pound man in first-rate shape fear a hundred pound beast? And intelligence certainly helps determine the victor."

"The chimpanzee is the only pragmatic exception," Rabun interrupted. "I've done research with chimps and one weighing barely over a hundred pounds, whether male or female, could easily maul the biggest NFL linebacker."

"No shit?" Warlock was temporarily stunned with this wonderful piece of information. It was simple to imagine Cosell announcing such a battle, and the nasalated howl when the chimp tore off the linebacker's face. Then he sensed he was losing the argument and rose to the challenge. "Few use chimps as a substitute for guard dogs."

"I seriously considered it," Rabun replied. "The weather is too coarse up here and the pulmonary problems would drive one crazy. There is the additional problem that chimpanzees cannot adapt to our environment any better than Indians and blacks. Chimps take readily to smoking, drinking, drug addiction . . ."

"How appalling." Diana turned on them. "You pitiful pigs. First you're killing dogs, fighting chimpanzees, then slandering blacks and Indians. I'm going home."

30

Business was slow; that was the problem. He longed for the crazed adrenal rush of his spadework in the Upper Peninsula; the great dark forests and solitary nights, not to speak of the steaming Aurora. Memory played tricks when bogged down in paperwork. The kitchen table seemed to buckle under the piles of audits, and he dreaded the phone calls from Feingold. Rabun was deep in the creation of some new gizmo and didn't want to be bothered, other than to complain about the spending habits of his wife and son. There had been the promise of a foray against a Chrysler dealership in Kansas, jointly owned by Rabun and a cousin; plane tickets had been purchased, a suitcase carefully packed. Warlock had always heard that Sweden was the Kansas of Europe, which he translated as meaning that Kansas was the Sweden of United States, missing the joke. Feingold had called at the last minute to say that it had been decided to bankrupt the dealership. Warlock hated the idea that Feingold had his phone number but Rabun had insisted. This temporarily gave the lawyer the upper hand.

"Never call me during dinner hour, Feingold."

"I will if the matter is sufficiently important. In the city we eat at a more sophisticated hour."

"You eat shit, kiddo. So does Detroit. Restaurantwise, the whole city sucks shit through a dirty sock."

"My god, what a repulsive remark. How about the London Chop House?"

"The exception proves the rule." Warlock had always considered this idea to be fatuous. "All I'm saying is don't call during dinner or you might find yourself out of work."

"I doubt you would have that much pull with my law firm. It's a big operation."

"I'm good at digging up the dirt, buster. I can tell by your voice you're into weird sex, double dealings, probably hard drugs like cocaine which is a big thing with you legal jet setters."

"I won't be threatened, you hick," Feingold interrupted. "I've done nothing wrong."

"Never said you did. I'll frame you. Say stuff some coke in your wife's purse at Hudson's, then tip the police. Think of the embarassment. . . ."

"I'm not married!" Feingold yelled triumphantly.

"Calm down. Then what I'll do is hire a boy to testify to the police that you sodomized him so badly he couldn't play basketball for a week. Get the picture?"

"Why would you do such an awful thing? You're crazy."

"To get you to stop calling while I'm eating dinner. Do we have a deal?"

"Okay, okay. Are you some sort of a gourmet cook?"

"You might say that."

Warlock had taken Clete along for a one day raid on a shipping pallet manufacturing firm over near Alpena. He

didn't want to carry a gun and Alpena was an area renowned
for roughnecks; true, he felt he was three quarters honed steel
but the last quarter could be a fatal margin and Clete was a
retired champion street fighter. Clete also looked like he belonged in northern Michigan while Warlock could not bear to
subdue his tailoring to that extent. The case was simple: an
audit had revealed a pathetically obvious kickback scheme
where far too much was being paid for the raw lumber to make
the shipping pallets. They had lunch with a dumpy little man
who served as a buyer. Clete masqueraded as timber foreman
and Warlock as a sawmill owner. After the buyer had gulped
a number of Manhattans while fiddling with his string tie, he
made his criminal proposal. Warlock left the table and called
the plant manager who came over and fired the culprit on the
spot. It was an easy day's work though Warlock recognized his
commission net would be small. The dumpy little man sniveled
a great deal about his children as the police led him away. It
was terribly unpleasant and Clete went up to the bar and drank
a great deal.

"Thanks a lot, Clete," Warlock said, joining him. "It was an
easy case. I'd like to split the commission with you." His heart
warmed again after the sobs of the dumpy little man moved
out of range.

"Stuff it up your dead ass," Clete said with vehemence.

"Geez, what did I do?" Warlock was shocked.

"How do you know the plant manager wasn't involved? Or
the accountants? That poor little shit will spend the holidays
in jail taking a fall for the others. Use your head."

"I guess I jumped the gun. We had him dead to rights. He
was guilty as shit. You're just saying others might be guilty, too."

"Let's get the fuck out of here."

*   *   *

The wound had healed a bit between the old friends during a few days of deer hunting with a new acquaintance of Warlock's, met while jogging through the woods. He jogged only in the woods out of the sight of the curious because he thought the activity faddish and banal. The rough terrain will build me the legs of a halfback, he thought, one golden October afternoon far out in the woods. There was a shotgun explosion in the direction Hudley had run and Warlock had dived briefly for cover, then remembered it was grouse hunting season. He found a man sitting on a stump in a clearing examining a large, dead grouse, while Hudley was mounting the man's bird dog in a frenzy.

"Sorry," Warlock apologized, waving at Hudley. He recognized the man as a redheaded, hard drinking local businessman named Hank. They shook hands.

"It's fine by me. My dog is a male, too."

"Jesus. Hud always goes after the ladies."

"Your dog is bisexual," Hank said, drawing two warmish beers from the pockets of his capacious hunting coat. "Or maybe today he's discovered he's a fagola."

"I don't get it." Warlock drank deeply from the warm beer, feeling a smidgin of insult, but also the inherent advantage of Hank carrying a shotgun.

"There's nothing to get. So your dog's a fag. So what? Skiiers are fags. So are tennis players. So are politicians. So are most joggers."

"See here . . ."

"No, see here. This is my land and your dog is raping my dog. I could have him thrown in jail."

"I wonder if there are many prosecuted cases of dog rape." Warlock sensed and was warming to Hank's irrational jests.

"It's not really my land. I need a cold beer."

They ended up traveling cross-country to Hank's house, broiling two grouse which they basted with lemon, butter and thyme. And deer hunting with Clete a few weeks later substantiated the alliance based on Hank's interest in sporting art. They shot an illegal doe and ate a great deal of it at Clete's, washed down with his favorite wine, which was whiskey. Warlock brought home a hindquarter to Diana, who loved venison. She was pleased with this new outside interest of Warlock's, having since youth despised the sensation of clinging.

The day before Thanksgiving he came down with a horrid form of the flu that put both ends of his feverish body into action. He wept with disappointment in the toilet. Their bags were packed for the annual trip to Diana's father's farm outside of Eaton Rapids: the trip, never missed in nearly ten years of marriage, was to be an agreed upon parole from the rigors of diet. For days he imagined and remembered the bounty of her parents' table and the merriment of children and the gaggle of grandchildren. He had even bought a new suit, and loved the idea of secretively referring to his new prosperity to her father and brothers who, after a period of suspicious probation, had enjoyed Warlock. After all, Little D., as they called her, was very happy and that was the main thing.

"Maybe I should stay with you, darling," Diana said through the door.

"Nothing doing. A sick dog wants to be alone." Hearing the front door click brought a subdued sob of self-pity, with nauseating turkey and ham whirling behind his clenched eyes. He dozed on the toilet rug, dreaming that the forbidden herring he had eaten were herring that had witnessed the *Titanic* coming down through the water, with drowning bodies of her passengers following, tumbling end over end in tuxedoes and gowns. Warlock answered the phone on the seventeenth audible ring.

31

Death when it came, came all at once, like a soap bubble bursting, he thought, picking up the phone. It better not be that jerk Feingold.

"There's been an accident." It was Rabun.

"Oh my god! Diana!" He felt a new surge of nausea.

"No, not Diana. In the health spa I own in Florida. I'm being sued for a million dollars over my liability limit. . . ."

"I got a temperature of a hundred and one and a half. I got flu," Warlock interrupted.

"You what! I'm talking about a million bucks and you're bringing up a sneeze. I'll see you at noon tomorrow."

"That's Thanksgiving. And I'm puking all the time, plus number two every few minutes. I'll mess up my car."

"I presume your car has a door. Just do your little business in the ditch. I'll give you a shot."

"Yes, sir. Rabun."

Crimenently! He took his favorite blanket and pillow into the bathroom in preparation for his vigil. Maybe he would be sick forever, like Mom. At least I am losing weight; that was the only bright side. Perhaps Diana should have stayed just in case of a coma. Hudley was not likely to run and fetch the neighbors. For some reason his brain summoned up the smell of canned dog food, then the odor of the Air Force mess steam table. This precipitated another double whammy with the attendant indecision of whether to hit the sink or toilet first. Neither, then the belated three steps between both. Oh my god, my dear pillow soiled. Why have you forsaken me.

His intermittent sleep was favored by brilliantly livid dreams of sex, power, triumph. In one segment he had dozens of brothers and sisters, something he had always longed for as an only child. There was a beautiful brunette nurse in suspenders and another glimmer of the future with fish swimming in the air with smiles, a war club and a pelt of scalps. There was a windstorm near dawn and a dream of King Arthur and Merlin from "The Book House," crying out in a swamp, but it was Hudley crying about the windstorm.

At Rabun's Warlock shook hands with a huge man with a small voice, then ran for the toilet. He actually didn't have to go but wanted to demonstrate how put out he was by the summons. He felt built out of raw rubber tubes; thin, pale, wan, a feeling somehow not corroborated by the mirror. He stood there flushing the toilet every few minutes, making sinister faces, and thinking that his stomach was hideously raw but he might have to pick at something if it was a lunch meeting. Rabun tapped at the locked door.

"Let me in. I have your shot."

"Okay," Warlock groaned. "It better help." He undid his pants to validate the charade, and opened the door.

"In minutes you'll feel the best you ever have." Rabun jammed the needle of a massive hypodermic into Warlock's ass.

"Jesus!" he roared.

"I'm a little rusty. This is my own secret concoction."

Warlock had barely made it back to the living room when a shimmering, golden power seized his body; a sense of ease, grace, strength. The stranger turned out to be the dreaded phone maven, Feingold, who presented Warlock with a wheel of Stilton cheese shipped straight from Harrods in London.

"A peace offering. Why don't you just take your phone off the hook during dinner?"

"Swell idea. Thank you." Warlock stared happily at his favorite cheese. "You sound small on the phone. God, Rabun, what the fuck was in that shot?"

"I can't tell you. You might become a drug addict. I limit myself to one a month."

"I must know," Warlock insisted with a false note of petulance. He had the sensation that he could jump straight through the ceiling into the open sky above.

"Well, Feingold flew up for an hour and I wanted you cooking on all cylinders. The concoction includes an antispasmodic, morphine, Nembutal, cocaine, Methedrine, and an enormous amount of B-12."

"You should patent it. What a boon it would be for the sick."

"You can buy all the ingredients on the street in Detroit," Feingold quipped. "I've read that they're giving something similar to terminal cancer patients in England."

"Are you suggesting that I have cancer?" Warlock turned in anger on Feingold, then looked questioningly at Rabun.

"Who knows? However, cancer isn't the subject of the meeting today."

Hours later they had made enough progress for Feingold to leave. Warlock decided that he had severely underestimated the man's intelligence, though there was a slight air of the supercilious nosepicker. The health spa lawsuit was actually the last of three central problems as far as cash outflow, the other two being Rabun's wife and son. Feingold was fairly certain that any settlement would fall within Rabun's liability limits. The spending habits of mom and son were humiliatingly perverse to the three of them. There was a two hundred percent cost overrun on Mrs. Rabun's new house, and the son was demanding a quarter mil to start a restaurant in Key West. There was implication of threat in the son's request, with overtones of knowledge of some of Rabun's tax shenanigans.

"That little cocksucker must have snooped in my files. I'm going to have him permanently locked in a closet. He's a bigger bitch than his mother." Rabun stomped around in his balloon boots. "Why couldn't my son turn out to be an android football player or something normal. No, he's down there in the tropics playing with weenies."

"At least he hasn't murdered anyone." Warlock searched for a shred of condolence.

"I've seen a lot worse." Feingold offered his ancient wisdom, rolling his eyes at Warlock as Rabun threw an alabaster peach through the picture window. Then Rabun grabbed Warlock by the lapels.

"Do something about this mess, you hear? I'm on the verge of the greatest discovery of my career. I'm getting old, and my brain is being trampled by cunts and perverts. I beg you."

"I will, sir. I promise it on my life." His eyes grew misty at the solemnity of the moment.

Warlock had to walk Feingold out to his rent-a-car to protect him from the not imaginary threat of the dogs.

"If you do anything illegal don't tell me about it. Lawyers have a code of ethics."

"Yeah, that's why they do so well in politics." He felt himself toughening for the big mission.

"Since you so obviously enjoy snooping around you might do a head count at the motel and a boat count at the marina. Actually I'm jealous. I know a lot of ladies in Lauderdale. You want some phone numbers?"

"I'll do it my way," Warlock said sententiously. "I never buy a pig in a poke." What was a poke?

Rabun's tantrum had passed leaving him in a state of serene melancholy. They split a roast pheasant and a bottle of 1953 Richebourg.

"My compliments to the chef wherever she is." The effects of the drug concoction were beginning to wear off.

"I do my own cooking."

"You don't!" He was astounded. This surely was a Renaissance man.

"I do. It's primarily a diagnostic and prognostic situation, a matter of textures and odors, a comprehension of the physical nature of the material."

"I cook but not this well."

"Diana told me you did. I judge the sensitivity of a man by what he eats and who he fucks." Rabun winked and laughed.

"Sometimes we backslide a little bit." Warlock was thinking of Aurora.

"Of course we do. Haute cuisine would be a bore without

variation. I occasionally make myself a hamburger or a pot of chili. Most nurses are hamburgers, frankly. You're very fortunate to be married to a ruffed grouse."

"Thank you." They toasted and Warlock reminded himself to share this wonderful compliment with Diana.

32

What wretchedness! Warlock barely made the house before another double entendre struck with ponderous violence, as if in its flip-flops his body was rejecting all of the amplitude beneath the skin. Why was there flu on earth? Hot tears of injustice fell on his bare thighs. And there should be laws against the drugs that dropped one so violently from so high a perch. It was like a fucking airplane crash. Perhaps Rabun was mad as a hatter; he was certainly eccentric past acceptable bounds. Dad used to say that one half the population was always peeing in the pool that the other half had to swim in. It anyway would be a good while before he could face another pheasant.

By midnight his system had calmed down enough to allow him to take out his briefcase and sort the new batch of information. His concentration was shaky so he studied his favorite book of all, the Rand McNally road atlas. There was Florida hanging like a cumbersome dick down into the ocean; the association was unpleasant, but back in the old high school library some joker always defaced the Florida map into a dick.

The girls would shriek when they hit that page, likely with false modesty as most of them were farm girls. There was an image of the most winsome girl in his 4-H group leading her heifer out to a tethered bull who was bellowing and blowing snot out of his nose, his ruby flag at full mast.

On his single vacation trip to Florida with Diana they had both thought the state to be imponderably sleazy outside a few locations, say the Everglades, an afternoon in the Flagler Museum in Palm Beach, and the ocean itself. So much of the trip had been unpleasant: on the charterboat the mate had clubbed the huge amberjack to death when Warlock wanted the fish released back to his watery home, and the captain was pissed when he wouldn't pay to have the fish mounted—who wanted a big, dead fish in his house; even worse were the ghastly college kids on the beach in front of their Fort Lauderdale hotel. The boys would gather their blankets in an island around Diana's, neglecting their own kind. Their jack-off leers repulsed Warlock and fueled his jealousy to the extent that he finally confined his wife to the hotel pool. The quarrel lasted for days —Diana preferred the ocean. He had felt so badly that he began to think that his divorce from Marilyn had been, career-wise, changing horses in midstream, an unthinkable act to even the most otiose cowboy. But then the cowboy wasn't married to Marilyn with her nasty logic and vaunting social ambitions in East Lansing. Her inauguration into the local Junior League turned her into Princess Margaret; her accent changed and her clothing budget soared. A close quartered confrontation with Marilyn could be likened to being rolled up tightly in a cold, wet wool blanket; the heart and brain choking on their own grimly altered juices as the argument prolonged itself. Then the fated, foreordained meeting with Diana after his Economics Club speech: good sense disintegrated like shards of frozen manure in the face of the power of love at first sight. After their second, secretive date they had tried to go all the way in his modest compact car on a lover's lane; her pearlish mellow laughter rang out in the June night air at his improbable maneuvers. She had suggested a motel for the next meeting, then had headed down on him with a voluptuous energy that left him at evening's end with some kicked off radio and heater dials.

Warlock's eyes refocused on the map but now his wiener probed up through the red terry cloth robe: Diana was the ocean and his dick was Florida. He considered self-abuse, but suspected it might precipitate another wave of illness. Better to save it for his returning beloved, an essentially false Chinese notion of sexuality he had read but not believed. She was safe in the arms of her family, waiting to return to him. He suddenly remembered, then discarded a stoned fantasy she had confessed to wherein she had made love to a group of men and Warlock had emerged champion. He much preferred the notion that he could retain his crown without entering any competitions. He took a number ten Valium, fed Hudley a pound of partially thawed hamburger, locked the doors, left most of the lights on, and went to bed, a fresh pillowcase on his still vaguely odiferous, favorite pillow—a soft heirloom that swept him into the longest sleep of his life.

He began the day in the middle of the afternoon with a hearty cup of hot water. The weather was bad with snow and blustery winds; the wait for Diana became a vigil of loneliness and dark imaginings. Short of Siberia it was hard to find an area with worse weather than northern Michigan, where he had recently announced rather pompously he would "retire" with the air of a cinema Indian saying "Here I stand." The phone was on the blink from the weather and the TV loaded with late afternoon drivel; his stomach was too raw for a drink and the dog whined at the door but wouldn't go outside. Assuming Diana's safety, the Florida jaunt was a wonderful opportunity for action. He might have to beef up his hot weather wardrobe. Hudley made a strange humpback circle, a movement prefactory to pooping. The scoundrel. He grabbed the dog, opened the door and flung him off the porch steps, just grazing Diana who, head bent to the wind and snow, was coming toward him.

"Would you hit a woman with a dog?" She laughed.

"No. I guess I already did." The wind whipped his robe open. He embraced her and she stepped on a bare foot submerged in a pile of snow. It didn't matter, she was home. Hudley came back on the porch and made a not altogether playful pass at his robe.

In the kitchen she unpacked a sack containing a dozen Tupperware containers, while he rushed on in a litany of complaints about Rabun, his illness, the dog, Florida, his worries about her safety.

"But it was a beautiful day until the last fifteen miles, darling."

"No shit?" The Leelanau Peninsula pushed so far out into Lake Michigan that it often possessed weather totally peculiar to its geography. He made her a bullshot out of consommé and vodka, deciding the mixture looked healthy enough for him to try. It was like a chunk of cactus in his guts.

"The fucking flu has my whole body on the fritz." He poked into her Tupperware.

"Mom sent you a little of everything we had for dinner."

"I better wait for breakfast." His anger began to rise at his illness.

"It was an upsetting trip. She kept saying she had all four of her babies by my age. Everybody sided with her after they heard about your job, though I waffled a bit there. I said maybe in March we'd think about it if I don't get the scholarship."

"Bullshit!" Her sad, puzzled face seemed to demand an extreme position. "By March I'll be able to send you to medical school."

"But you said you wanted to buy a place instead of always renting." She enjoyed it when he became captious and marched around, blowing off steam like her father had always done when crop prices plummeted.

"An education is more important than a house. Any fuck-head can own a house. I've been thinking a lot about your ambitions. . . ."—a bold faced lie. "First things first. We can always adopt after medical school." The single, painful bullshot had slipped into his brainpan. "You've done so much for me. You saved my life. I love you too much to hold you back. You can't bury your talents."

"I hope you're not taking your pistol to Florida." She saw that he had hit an embarrassing, manic phase.

"Pistol? Pistol. Pistol. I don't need a pistol. Hit me in the gut. I'm hard as a rock. Hit me."

"After three days of flu," she smiled.

"Yeah, maybe not. Then feel my arms. Actually what I've been thinking is my dad fibbed and bullied the shit out of me back when I was on the track of the great Gauguin." Warlock sloppily poured another drink. "I was stupid enough to believe all his bullshit. Now you're going to give your mother a baby?"

"You're right, darling." She embraced him, feeling warm

but suspicious about his new generosity of spirit after he'd been badgering her off and on for years to have a baby. "But you used to admit that one reason you wanted a baby was so I wouldn't run off."

"I guess I remember that. I guess I've changed. I'm changing the future. I haven't told you about it yet." He began kneading the front of her wool skirt.

"You're what?" The new job had altered his behavior in ways that she had been too busy to give much notice to. "I don't understand."

"Suffice it to say that every day in a lot of little ways I'm changing the future." He reached around her to nab a finger full of turkey stuffing out of a container.

PART THREE

Ah, they must be seen, the masks people wear under our great opalescent skies, and when they walk and move, daubed with cruel colors, wretched and pitiful under the rain, bowing and fawning terrified figures at once insolent and timid, growling or yapping, with shrill falsetto voices or loud metallic voices, with the heads of macabre beasts and the unexpected, unsubdued gestures of irritated animals. Repulsive humanity ever on the move in cast-off clothes shimmering with spangles torn from the mask of the moon. Then I saw things in a big way and my heartbeat quickened and my bones trembled, and I divined the enormity of these distortions and anticipated the modern spirit. A new world loomed up before me.

JAMES ENSOR

33

The most successful travelers are those who have nurtured their sense of destiny, who believe that their presence on a plane has a positive, inevitable effect on the safety of the flight. Such a man was Warlock. He knew that a fuzzy self-image, a free floating sense of failure, were self-fulfilling prophesies. Put a hundred pessimistic fuck-ups on the same plane and the pilot is not getting any help. The will of man was an unplumbed mystery, he thought, high above Georgia, leafing through *Fortune* and regretting that he hadn't bought a skin magazine. There was an attractive girl in a bikini leaning over a computer, and that was it for the whole magazine, a fillip, like the show biz tarts occasionally offered in *Time,* the wonderful underwear ads in *The New York Times* Sunday magazine. Actually he would have gone for the skin but Feingold had met him with another folder when he changed to Delta at Detroit Metro. The snoopy prick had stayed plastered like a decal to him until they hit the boarding gate, thus it was *Forbes* and *Fortune* to prove his solidity.

It had been snowing hard and the waiting passengers seemed

to be making muffled puppy noises. Feingold shook his head.

"I wouldn't fly today for all the money in the world."

"Thanks, kid, but I could bribe you out of pocket onto that plane in ten seconds."

"Probably. All you north-woods geezers are big on cash. I'll be helping you with the IRS in a few years. Look, I insist you take this girl's number. I grew up with her. She's got great connections. A Jewish girl might pound some sense into you."

"Sense is for little minds. Out on the street you got to have instinct." He shrugged and accepted the number. "I've slept with a lot of your kind, Feingold. Nothing special." In real life, the life outside of his mind, Warlock had never gotten past first base (heavy petting) with a Jewish girl.

"You're lucky. I'm a Jew and I've never been past second base with one. That's bare tit. The girls my age got standards. An engagement ring turns the trick. The young ones are different, but youth is messy."

"Keep your pecker up. I'll call." Warlock had slapped him on the shoulder and got on the plane.

Despite all of this braggadocio there were certain problems, Warlock admitted. Taking off and landing are the dangerous times, and high over Georgia was the period to at least entertain the idea of difficulties. He hadn't been able to make reservations for the plane, accommodations, and special car rental. In desperation he had turned to Rabun's snazzy travel agent in New York. However distantly, this seemed to break cover. After two days of wonderful lovemaking—his slimmer tummy made for better contact, he noted—even Diana appeared to be jolly about sending him off. Bright girl that she was, it was her idea that he take the old beret along as a possible cover as an artist. She gave him guidebooks on shorebirds and

Florida restaurants. He extracted a late night promise that should she become a doctor, that wouldn't obviate the erotic use of nurse's uniforms and garter belts. But primary among his worries was Rabun himself: as Warlock became more and more successful, Rabun became more greedy and demanding. There was a last minute meeting on the way to the dawn plane at the Traverse City airport, and Diana hadn't been sufficiently out of earshot. Now, with the aid of several rum drinks Warlock's mind was a whirl of details about motels, the spa, the marina, Rabun's wife and son. And a phone call to Dad for hot tips had left an eerie knot in his stomach. Dad was vehemently dire and gave his son a group of phone numbers of powerful compatriots in Florida law enforcement. Now as the pilot announced their passage over invisible Jacksonville, Dad's words drove into his brain with the rhetorical power of John L. Lewis.

"Jesus, how the fuck you get yourself in these jams? Don't, I repeat, don't go to Florida. It's chocked full of detritus."

"I have to go, Dad. It's a commit." *Detritus* was an odd word for Dad to use.

"The place is full of murdering crooks, Cubans and Colombians wholesaling drugs with millions to spend. Your life isn't worth a plugged nickel down there. Why don't you get a job on construction and stick with your beautiful wife?"

"Construction wouldn't pay me the forty-five grand plus commission I get now," Warlock said proudly.

"Holy shit, you've got a sucker on the line. That's a lot more than I make. I'm going to bill you for advice. The best I can tell you is stay away from any Latins. They're behind all of this. We're not sure but we think Castro might be back there, too. Plus the Miami Jewish Mafia. You get what I mean? I don't want your ass shot off."

"None of my business is related to dope or Latins, Dad. And I think Mr. Castro is a little too busy running a country to get involved in dope."

"Everything's interconnected, kid. Don't forget it. Behind every Ivy League banker is a bubbling cesspool of shit. Everyone's on the take. That's why me and the little woman are retiring to Canada. Winnipeg to be exact."

"What's in Winnipeg?" Warlock couldn't focus on the locale.

"Winnipeggians. They're honest. The crime rate is almost nonexistent. It's a little chilly in winter but so what."

It was surprisingly blustery and chilly at the West Palm Beach airport, with one of those steady northeasters that hang on for weeks. They don't show the cold days in the photographs, he thought. Part of the glumness was the mute relief of surviving yet another subsonic hurtle across the sky, a mode of transportation not the less idiotic and frightening for being so prevalent.

An hour later he was sunk in a tub at his small suite at the Brazilian Court, studying his restaurant guide and drinking a room service rum punch. The desk clerk had assured him that a minor heat wave was beginning in the morning. The tancolored rental BMW was wonderful, with a spark that the poor Subaru would have envied.

Out of the tub he strode around in his robe, pondering the next move. He was bright enough to understand that reality was shot through with large empty spaces, spaces in which nothing whatsoever occurred. At his desk he laboriously marked out his key addresses on the map, turning to a state map to put a large, inane X on Key West. There was a minor sense of vertigo when he couldn't locate the Brazilian Court.

In order to get anyplace it was helpful to know where you were starting from. He would have liked to pin the maps to the wall to give the room the aura of a nerve center, but recognized the idea as imprudent. The place was not yet a home but a start had been made. He dressed for a stroll, then endured the manic indecision of putting on and taking off the beret a dozen times.

Within another hour he was deep, quite by accident, in the heart of the biggest part of his case. In a picturesque little arcade off Worth Avenue he came upon Mrs. Rabun's gallery. Warlock nearly blundered right in but hesitated, then stepped around the corner to counsel himself. Was he a playboy or a portraitist? Why not both to thicken the stew? He entered and assumed the studious, hands-behind-the-back attitude of the gallery habitué. He exchanged smiles with a tall, handsome woman in her forties, reading the Italian edition of *Vogue* behind the desk. One wall featured drawings of contemporary British artists—Hockney, Hepworth, Silkworth, et al. It was surprisingly tasteful, Warlock judged, though the other wall contained the meat and potatoes mishmash that supports a gallery, and a league of expensive interior decorators: seascapes, birdscapes, framed tapestries, chinoiserie, ballerinascapes.

"How cold is it out there?" She stared out at the gathering dark with a cardigan around her shoulders.

"Beats the hell out of the blizzard in Detroit."

"What a dreadful place." Her nostrils flared.

"Stopped there on the way down from Minneapolis." Why hadn't he prepared better?

"Excuse me but I have to close now." She handed him a card. "This place is hard to find."

"You're Nancy Rabun?"

"Yes. Unfortunately. It's cold and I'm bored."

"But you're lovely. I'll come by tomorrow and take another look at the Hockney." He tried to impart into his stare a slight suggestion of savage lust, of a possible undreamed of afternoon that would be the spiritual equivalent of a mud wallow. He turned to go as a blush rose to her cheeks.

34

Sometimes the only answer to death is lunch. The morning had been wickedly confusing, with the entire area failing to resemble the map. He had driven north on the island to reach Singer Island, the location of the marina, but when he had reached the Palm Beach inlet there was no bridge. His destination was only a hundred water yards away; in fact, Warlock could see the marina in question. He made the mistake of asking two little round-face snots fishing from the dock for directions. One grew very excited while the fatter of the two threw fishing sinkers at birds and, oddly, drank from a pint bottle of French olive oil.

"You can't get there except to swim and this place is loaded with sharks. We pushed this German shepherd off the dock yesterday and the sharks ate him in no time flat."

"Surely you can drive there. In fact I can see cars from here." The presence of sharks was startling and he stared deeply into the water.

"I'm not old enough to drive. I'll give you five bucks if you eat this," he said, throwing a large chunk of rotten bait at his friend. The friend put down his sinkers and olive oil and took a tentative sniff of the prize.

"We never been over there," the fat one said, as Warlock walked back to his car, not wanting to see the kid eat the fish. Youth, like adulthood, was full of economic cruelties. Unless he was a thief, the fat kid must pay plenty for his olive oil fix.

Rabun's motel down near Lantana on A1A was relatively simple in that it entailed a straight line south from his vision of Singer Island. He went into the lobby and inquired about March reservations and was surprised to find out that they were booked solid after January first. That made those months easy to check with the CPA, but didn't free a possible coverup in December. He took a brochure that included a room map and went back to the car. On the far side of the road was mostly a nasty mangrove swamp, except for a small clearing where a man sold fruit from a semitrailer. The prospects for comfortable spying were small. Now he recognized that he should have gone for something less noticeable than a tannish-colored BMW. He bought a sack of oranges from the surly Italian that manned the truck; but then the man spoke Spanish to an old woman who assisted him. Cuban. He must avoid clichés like Italian fruit vendors.

The health spa was located on the road to the Wellington Polo Grounds. It was an imposing stucco building, a windowless cube that led one to suspect the occupants were up to no good. So this is where Mrs. Bob Fardel of North County Road suffered irreparable spinal injuries at the hands of a berserk exercise machine? His lip curled with cynicism, imagining the litter of venal lawyers behind the case; the world had become a litigious nightmare, with every driver a potential whiplash supplicant. He would no doubt find the cunt doing cartwheels on her back lawn, behind a shrubbery hedge that would be difficult but not impossible for him to penetrate. It was the age-old question of the right man for the right job. He laid a little rubber out of the parking lot for no particular reason. It was barely after eleven but he was definitely peckish. There were two more possible stops on the map—the architect and the construction company for Mrs. Rabun's house—but his body felt swept with fatigue, and there was the gesture of leaving something to do in the afternoon.

Back in his quarters he was struck head on by the problem of loneliness, and what it can do to a borderline neurotic. An orange had temporarily allayed his hunger and he sat at the desk puzzled by the quaver in his mind, heart and bowels. A month ago Dad had sent him *Employee Theft Investigation* by J. Kirk Barefoot (not a nom de plume; this fascinating study may be ordered from Butterworth Books, 10 Tower Office, Woburn, MASS. 01801). But not even Barefoot could distract him from a rising tightness in his chest, a peculiar lightness midway between the ears. He identified the sensation finally as the dread sister of the anxiety attack he had suffered in Sault Ste. Marie.

As usual, the sufferer in these circumstances is blind to the help at hand: the ocean was a mere five blocks away, fine restaurants even closer, women that were susceptible to a proposal were an easy half mile across Lake Worth in West Palm Beach, even something so simple as a purchase of clothing would have staved off the attack. In short, swim, eat, fuck, buy; return to reality, embrace it, O anchorite of crime. Run from the rooms whose walls have already begun to move. You can't balance the whole earth herself on your puny nose. Run.

Instead he rifled through the desk, discovering a number of

fairly recent *Reader's Digest*'s, Mom's favorite magazine in the old days, to the point that she subscribed to the Condensed Book series. Warlock checked out the "Life in These United States" section for the sort of joke that can change a day. No luck. There was an article on contemporary marital fidelity excerpted from *Psychology Today* with the unlikely title of "Is What Is Good for Peter, Good for Petra?" A Greek couple, he wondered, but reading on saw that the piece applied readily to Paul and Paula, Gene and Janine, George and Georgette. The changing tides of fidelity swept through his mind, from full froth to neat neap, from the moon's fulsome spring tide to a fishing boat tipped sideways in the Bay of Fundy's mud. Some wives paid wayward husbands back tit for tat, and some new wave types frittered through life as Don Juanettes. Warlock hastily compared the evident loss of standards to the lack of the old Dickensenian faithfulness in employees evidenced in Barefoot's book.

By the end of the article tears begin to form at the thought that Diana might ever step out on him. To be sure, the lady was highly sexed, but he wasn't a shirker when it came to satisfying her. Barring illness, he had never turned her down and she would vouch for this. The angle of tit for tat was bothersome, but Patty's blowjob in the bowling alley parking lot couldn't be held against him. It was obviously up in the air whether a blowjob constituted adultery in the first place, the Bible making no mention of the act. Rules had to be laid down in some form. The distant night in Corona, and the more recent three day session with Aurora up in Sault Ste. Marie, presented more severe difficulties to his waffling spirit. Diana in a weak moment had once said she could forgive him for a one night stand with a lady of the night if he were drunk. He tried mightily to remember being drunk throughout the three days with Aurora. All of those years of going to Sunday school at the Congregational Church bore down on him like a descending ceiling in a spy film. He was dangerously close to prayer but could only remember the words to "Now I lay me down to sleep," and "Bless all the children throughout the world who are cold, sick or hungry." Or all three. They kept changing the translation of the Lord's Prayer and he anyway couldn't remember the whole thing.

After an hour or so of this self-defeating nonsense his muscles finally tightened in arrogance in the bathroom. He failed to find a Valium in his kit but there was a big bomber with a ribbon tied around it, a joke gift from Diana. Hadn't she understood the rigidity of airport security? May as well take a big draw on the sucker to aid the appetite. He put on a bathing suit just in case, then a Hawaiian shirt, and loose white linen trousers. Quite the sport. And a pale gray linen jacket.

"My, haven't you gone tropic," Mrs. Rabun said. Again, Warlock was the only customer in the gallery. Was there an edge of jest in her voice?

"I actually dreamt about the Hockney. I must have it." He was stoned and giddy as a monkey.

"I'm not sure. I sell things so infrequently that I hate to let them go."

"Oh, come now." She looked somehow sedate and yummy at the same time. One mustn't forget the needs of the mature woman, he thought, forgetting in a trice the recent horror of adultery.

"Okay. I mean I know I'm being captious. Would you like me to have it framed?"

"Not necessary. I'll frame it myself. I'll pick it up after lunch and the beach." There was a dangerous quasislur between "lunch" and "beach." He liked the idea of this woman using the word "captious."

"Are you an artist?" She was amused at his evident goofiness.

"I used to be a portraitist."

"I loathe portraitists. They're lying shits." She was vehement.

"That's why I quit. Then I went on the trail of the great Gauguin." They were interrupted by a gay blade, an obvious friend of Mrs. Rabun's.

"He bought the Hockney," she said.

"Oh not the Hockney. Not the Hockney. The Hockney. I loved it. Not the Hockney. How could you, you bastard. Not the Hockney."

35

The real trouble with walking a long ways is that you usually have to walk back. But the beach was resplendent with a warm, moist wind from the south; and nearly unoccupied, which was a puzzle. Since these rich people were so close to the ocean, they no doubt all had pools to show they didn't need the ocean. Warlock was still a trifle stoned and felt a special kinship with the sea; probably, he thought, because Dad and my uncles were all Navy men in World War II. To be sure, that ocean, the Pacific, lay well to the west but they supposedly merged in the Panama Canal, and south of South America and north of North America. That was the problem with dope: everything came together for a short while, but then it fell apart again. Dad always advised him to get "high on life" but then Dad was quite a drinker. Dad had also said that "the hobo is a sunshine millionaire."

About fifty yards down the beach two children were playing in the moderate surf, watched over by a woman in a wheelchair and a large black maid. There was a lavender parasol above the wheelchair and a Chinese kite tail hanging from it fluttered in the wind. A group of sanderlings skittered by narrowly avoiding each wave wash, at which point they dashed after the receding water, pecking in the sand for marine organisms. A shudder of absolute peace swept over him but only briefly. He wanted to go swimming, but where would he put his billfold? Not impossible. He undressed down to his bathing suit and backed slowly into the water, glancing seaward with an obtuse desire for direction. With a little wit, problems could be solved. Then his heel caught on a coral outcropping and he tripped, grasping wildly at the air for a handhold. Oh well. Hopefully too shallow for sharks. He surfaced, feeling foolish without witnesses, and rubbed the salt water from his face, momentarily disoriented. Where the fuck is the land? There it is, with my clothes on it. Then there was a truly memorable chorus of screams from down the beach. The black maid was struggling with the wheelchair which had tipped over and the two children were running in noisy circles.

Warlock reached them in no time flat, wallowing out of the water and breaking into a sprint. The maid wept along with the little girl while the boy stood there whitefaced, trying to figure out the situation. One of the wheels had slipped off the walkway. Warlock knelt by the woman as she laughed and struggled to her elbows. He brushed sand from her face and sandy colored hair. Her white nightie was twisted around her body and her afghan had slipped to her knees revealing a bare bottom that had few equals on earth.

"May I help?"

"I should hope you can. You could right the chair and lift me into it. Or carry me up the walk. Or cover any exposed parts." She was still laughing. "Hannah, Jeanette! Stop crying or mother's going to shoot you. Leighton, get the wheelchair on the walk."

"Righto." Warlock reached down her body and straightened her nightie, which was semitransparent, so he pulled the afghan up over her bottom.

"You don't have to be tender. Please just get me out of this goddamn sandbox."

He lifted her easily and, liking the feeling, carried her up the walkway and into a garden surrounding a swimming pool.

"Here's okay." She gestured to a chaise longue. He laid her gently down and made a perhaps unnecessarily prolonged attempt to straighten her nightie and afghan. He had avoided looking into her eyes, not wanting to trip.

"There you are. I better get back. I left my billfold in my trousers." He looked into her eyes and felt a blush rise. She was onto his lame but excusable nursing efforts.

"Leighton will get your clothes. There are very few pickpockets on our beaches. I'm Laura. You have this strange accent. May I guess rural Indiana?" She pressed a buzzer on a wicker table beside her, and patted the longue for him to sit down.

"Johnny, Michigan." He offered his hand then started to withdraw it.

"It's everything below my breasts. I had an accident a few months ago." A black man in a waiter's coat appeared and she ordered drinks. The children and maid appeared as if by magic with his clothes. The old black woman was still distraught and Laura kissed her hand and dismissed them all. "That's okay, honey, nobody's at fault." They wandered off and Laura whispered in an aside, "She's been with me since I was born. She's totally incompetent but then so is everyone else on earth."

"I'm very sorry about your injury," Warlock said in a hoarse whisper. Outside of Diana she was the most beautiful woman he had ever seen, and about the same age. Her husky southern accent hit him hard below the waist for some reason and there was a little shame in this sexual attraction to paralysis. How could he? The evidence coiled and moved in his bathing suit, as if some hibernating reptile were feeling in a dark lair the first rays of spring sunshine. She had rearranged the afghan in an expansive swipe of her hand to the point that he felt compelled to concentrate on her face, with only a flicker or two below. The butler trundled up with a drink cart similar to those used on airplanes.

"My husband is interested in the machinery of alcohol. Help yourself. I'll have a gin and tonic, heavy on the gin."

"Will there be anything else, Mrs. Fardel?" The butler backed away slowly, missing by years of experience the edge of the swimming pool.

The name Fardel lit up like a forty watt bulb as he made the drinks, then exploded in the manner of an unpunctured baked potato in a hot oven. Oh my god! His mind raced back to the coincidences found in Dr. Zhivago that last spring of graduate school; the palms became linden trees, the lowering tropical sun shown on the Baltic outside St. Petersburg, rather than the Atlantic off Palm Beach. Laura looked like Julie Christie, only better.

"You're off in dreamland. What do you do?"

"I'm an artist . . . in a way," he stuttered. There was the temptation to continue the Russian theme, fall on his knees and weep that he was sent here to spy upon her.

"Must be a small way. There aren't any artists around here. I knew one real well but he went and jumped off this old bridge in New Orleans when I wouldn't be his mistress. There must have been extenuating circumstances, don't you think? No one commits suicide for love."

"Yes, they do. I can imagine dying for love." He had gulped his bourbon and got up to make another drink. "He must have been a sensitive soul and couldn't live without you."

"He was ugly drunk." She laughed. "Is that for me?"

"That what?" He looked around, sneaking another peak at her barely covered, delicate sparrow's nest.

"That." She pointed at the front of his bathing suit and the protuberant boner that stuck out against the material in the usual silly way. Forty-five degrees and confined.

"You might say that." He covered himself with a hand and sat down. How could he forget such a key item?

"You must be a kinky ole artist to get aroused over a cripple lady." She put the afghan over his lap in a mock horror.

"I better get going. It's a long walk to Brazilian Court." That had to be her hand, he thought, staring at a parrot up in a palm tree. "May I visit you sometime?" She had worked the suit open.

"Why, yes. It would be flattering. You seem a little goofy but then it might be the Indiana style."

"Michigan." He reached out and touched a breast, then moved his hand downward. There was the question of whether she could feel anything, but he could.

"I wish it wasn't daylight, dammit." Her hand moved with superlative deftness. "If it was dark you could stand up and shove that thing plumb in my mouth."

Bam. That was it. His legs shot out straight and rigid; he slid off the edge of the chaise with a groan. She barely let go or she would have tipped over again. They were quiet for a while, with Laura running her fingers through his damp hair. She lit a cigarette and he watched the sanderlings down on the beach to the clink of the ice in her glass.

"That's simply the most romantic thing I've ever done." She was laughing again.

Warlock turned and rearranged himself on his knees. He kissed her deeply with tears in his eyes.

36

He awoke with a start at midnight from the aftereffect of an acrid bourbon belch; searing polymers, and eardrums taut from listening to dreams. An author had called dreams "soul chasers," he remembered.

Linen certainly didn't hold a press, especially if you slept in it; his cuff buttons had imprinted his face with three red welts, and his fingers traced the scars before the mirror. The mark of Cain? He smiled the sardonic smile of the survivor: he had one of those rare strong hangovers, not strong in pain, but strong in the sense that he felt strong. Strong was the only word for it. In the shower her deep fated laughter replayed its somber music. Laura. Her name now stood for the glitter of the tropic moon they had watched, a moon as plump as a steamed mussel above the Atlantic.

"Did you see it move?" he had asked.

"Yes, darling. I've always been a moon and cloud watcher. I always think of Baudelaire's poem about clouds—

> *Le regard singulier d'une femme galante*
> *Qui se glisse vers nous comme le rayon blanc*

Que la lune onduleuse envoie au lac tremblant,
Quand elle y veut baigner sa beauté nonchalante.

"That's wonderful." He didn't really understand a word of
it but he was in that rare mood of the utterly untaught, who
have a certain feeling that they can play the piano.

The number of their shared likes and dislikes was extraordinary. She was a food expert though they continued drinking
through the dinner hour. Even more striking was her knowledge of and love for the great Gauguin. After Madeira she had
graduated from Pratt Institute, then returned to New Orleans
and jumping horses, convinced that her talent was insufficient
to bear her girlish ambitions. He became maudlin when they
turned to her injury, toward which she owned a biblical attitude: a cable on an exercise machine had snapped, stretching
her unmercifully. There was still a long shot that she might
partially recover; she would know within a month. He asked
her for a definition of "central cord sparing" which she had
used several times, along with "substantia gelatinosa."

"It means"—she lit a citronella candle and laughed—"that
I can still feel down here." She lifted her nightie with a flick
of her fingertips. The evening had been cool enough for her to
wrap the afghan around her shoulders. "It's the only place I can
feel the weather." The wobbling light was a mysterious beacon
on her pubis. His knees shook as he knelt.

"It must be strange having the Bermuda Triangle right in
your front yard." His voice quavered with nervousness.

"What an odd thing to say. It's all nonsense." She exhaled,
laughing as his fingers probed.

"This upper left-hand corner is Bermuda, and the other
upper corner is the Bahamas. And right here we're smack dab

in Palm Beach." O my kingdom for a half-foot tongue, he thought, I could levitate her. She made a particular noise as all women do, a signature: hers was a keening sound, as if a witch were caught under a fallen tree far out in some fog-shrouded forest and hadn't yet mustered the magic to free herself, or himself.

"Pull me down a little bit, and turn me over," she whispered.

"Carimba," he whispered, back in his room in a dark tropical suit. "If this be adultery, so be it"—not comprehending that a man in a questionable moral situation is given to pompous stands. Downstairs he inquired of the night bellman where he might get a substantial late night snack. The man was black so Warlock mentioned a hankering after barbecue.

"Not sending you to a barbecue shack. Nosiree. Nobody from here goes to no barbecue shack. You get yourself in troubles."

"Nonsense, my hands are registered throughout the Midwest. . . ." He tried a weak jest.

"Don't care about your hands, son. I ain't being responsible for no guest going to no barbecue shack. I'll go back and sneak in the kitchen and make you a nice sliced cucumber and mayonnaise sandwich. I even cut the crusts off."

"Here's a fucking cucumber for you, gramps." He passed the old man a fifty when something less would have done. Warlock got the address.

On the way to West Palm Beach he reflected there was a great deal of *Gone With the Wind* shuffle to local blacks. Up until the late fifties, Laura said, the blacks towed tourists around in the hot sun in rickshaws. In the cities of the north it was best to be ubiquitously polite. How strong and bright and healthy the rich were; throw in obtuse, venal and paranoid to complete the picture. Marilyn's father had ranted ad nauseum about the lazy poor to the extent that one imagined them encircling his Bloomfield Hills palace like a wagon train. Spread the goodies or you get it in the gizzard, his university poli sci teacher had said, a rowdy harbinger of the hip teachers of the sixties, who later peopled the religio-ecstasy cults of the seventies, and now were at the forefront of the wood stove revolution.

The blacks of West Palm Beach were of a different, more surly color. In the half-filled restaurant a drunk had pointed a finger and yelled bang bang bang. Warlock lit a cigarette and concentrated on the menu. There was a definite stiffening in the atmosphere and he wondered if he weren't simply bothering these people for no good reason. Except hunger. The waiter-cook was built like a sumo wrestler, a wonderful specimen, and there was the urge to follow the man's example. He ordered beer, beef and pork ribs, hamhocks and greens, baked beans and a side of raw sliced onion.

"You don't fuck around, do you?" the man said.

"Love has stolen my energy. I haven't eaten in recent memory." The drunk in the corner repeated louder bangs. "That man doesn't like me."

"He thinks you're a cop. You want your sauce mild, hot, hotter?"

"Hotter. Tell him I only bust businessmen." He wouldn't have worn the Haspel drip-dry and silk tie, but he intended to make a pass at the motel.

"William, shut your face," the waiter roared. "This man only busts businessmen. I'm the only one here so ease up."

The food was wonderful, he thought, during a long, almost vain attempt to find the motel. There was a streak of sauce on his tie but he fancied it resembled an abstract design of some sort.

He made last call at the motel bar—in fact, the bartender called out "last call" extra loud even though Warlock and an old wrangling couple were the only occupants. The bartender was guarded as Warlock laid out a crisp C-note, ordering a double for both of them. Does he think I'm a cop?

"Don't drink. Quit when I started here. Behind the bar you see what it does to people." He nodded at the old couple whose discussion seemed to rise to blows.

"Doesn't do shit to me. Two drinks a day, that's it." Warlock sometimes wondered where his dialogue came from. He hoped like an actor he was learning to swing with the situation. "Supposed to drive up to Fort Pierce, but I'm feeling tired. They got any room?" He yawned a phony yawn.

"Never. I been here two years and there's never a vacancy from the first of December until April. We got the fucking apple sauce and cottage cheese crowd. That's why my fucking tips are so small. They ought to raise the rates. These old fuckers are driving me up the wall. Had a party of six and they left me a quarter." The bartender punctuated his diatribes with vicious swipes of the counter with a wet rag.

"Shit. I got another hour behind the wheel." Presto, I got the information. He had come on a hunch and it paid off; better than renting and sitting in the fruit vendor's semi, spying on the place, which he had been considering. He tuned his hearing to the argument.

"Lyman, you keep drinking that beer and farting. You keep farting and you're going to sleep on the couch."

"I like beer," he stretched the "like" out into a silly whine.

"Beer stops you up. It always stops you up."

"Everything stops me up. It always has." Lyman exchanged glances with Warlock.

"If you'd walk with me in the morning you wouldn't be stopped up."

"You say herring stops you up. And you eat herring. I'm not walking on that goddamn beach." The old man sensed he had an audience. "I like sidewalks. Sidewalks used to be good enough for you before birds. Now you all the time want to look at birds. I don't give fuck-all for all these birds. I read birds are related to snakes. To me birds are just shitting snakes that shit on the pool furniture. . . ."

"I love it when you get angry, Lyman," she interrupted him, drinking deeply from a whiskey sour. "You've always been so attractive when you're angry. It brings so much life to your face."

37

Warlock drove away from the motel with the strident sense of having regained the world at large, a world where men acted instead of mulled, where men talked out loud and the colors of life were primary rather than muted and adumbrated; Dad's wonderful quote slipped into memory, the one where the admiral stood on the foredeck after a long hideous battle in the South Pacific, and spoke to his men: "Once and for all, men, we have belled the Nipponese cat." Now there was a basso, electrical pressure in his body—the protein rush from the barbecue was kicking in. Let the world have its puny mousse, its lighthearted quiches—there was an undeniable power in ribs and hamhocks. So much had happened since the dream, now five months back, that he seriously wondered if some secret power had been given him that summer solstice night in the forest. Had that knoll been the burial ground of ancient warriors and had his sleeping body osmotically sucked up their forgotten powers? Something definitely had happened. He had rid himself miraculously of the usual Protestant binge toward reducing one's spirits to the point that no life surprises are possible. There was a sudden image of climbing a tree outside of Laura's house and jumping like a giant flying squirrel from the tree through her open balcony window. At first light—after a night of love, he would somehow whisk her away to Michigan, where after successful surgery, Diana would nurse Laura back to health. The three of them would live happily in the old farmhouse. A queen or king sized bed would be in order. Think of them on a summer morn, cuddling in ignorant sleep while he dressed for some sort of manly work. The image made him gulp air in a hyperventilating frenzy. He put the BMW 320I through its paces, having no idea where he was, though the probability of Florida loomed strong. Bright lights, and a siren. His brothers in the cloth, the police.

"Jesus, I've been tailing this guy all the way from Minnesota." Warlock handed over his license and a number of hokum ID cards Dad had rigged for him.

"Geez, I didn't see anyone else." The patrolman was young and impressionable.

"You know better than to say that. I get too close and I'm burned. A month's effort out the fucking window." Warlock grew convinced of his despair.

"Sorry I screwed you up. Anything I can do to help?"

"The guy's a rich, left-wing gay out of Minneapolis. He's at the Breakers so I can pick him out tomorrow unless he skips."

"The Cockatoo." The patrolman was truly sorry, but this big deal had broken the boredom.

"The what?"

"Cockatoo. Mostly rich, mostly gay. After hours. Your only shot. I'll lead." The officer had transparently been overexposed to Joe Friday and Ben in his youth. Ben was now in the cold, cold ground.

Getting pulled over turned out to be a lucky break, he realized, in that the route back to civilization after the fantasy was long and tortuous. The cop slowed and waved good-bye in front of the Cockatoo. It was after three A.M. on a weekday but the parking lot was chocked with Rolls, Lamborghinis, Maseratis, and a rare mauve Daimler, a few pedestrian Mercedes; a single silver Husqvarna dirt bike was chained to a post with a silver chain.

There was a definite attempt to turn Warlock away in the foyer. The bouncers were twins, male and female, and both over two hundred pounds in garish punk outfits. But the single toilet marked Who Cares was close by and the decorator he had met at Mrs. Rabun's gallery was in the process of coming out of Who Cares.

"Hockney!" he screamed, embracing Warlock. "Are these assholes trying to keep you out of my club?" The bouncers cringed back against the cigarette machine as if hit across the upper lips with a crop. "We're all here. Gloria will be crazy to see you."

"I was a little lonely, you know, taking the night air." Warlock was led through the club, noting that it held the demimonde, no doubt providing a pressure valve for the swells.

"You've got a homing device, baby. You're in the right place."

Mrs. Rabun waved from a table around which sat a dozen male admirers. Warlock was introduced to the guest of honor, a purportedly important western artist. The artist leaned back in his chair with expensive cowboy boots—an eel and ostrich combo—resting on the tablecloth. His denim was faded and patched and his silver Zuni concho belt had torn a hole in the leather chair.

Finding Mrs. Rabun was a coincidence of not quite Zhivago importance. She kissed him effusively and rolled her cynical eyes at her audience and the table littered with magnums of vintage champagne—Ruinart, Cristal, Pérignon. Warlock figured she was picking up the tab for the mud bath. It wasn't hard to see where the money went.

"How about a rooty-toot-toot," his immediate neighbor on the left asked, pouring Warlock a lump of white powder and passing a silver straw.

"Paese che vai, usanza che trovi," he muttered, snorting the powder and catching Mrs. Rabun's eye. It was his sole Italian sentence and meant, vaguely, that it's best to go along with the crowd.

"You're full of surprises, dear Hockney." The nickname was sticking.

"Are you David Hockney, the Englishman? Your art sucks," said the western artist, jealous for attention. He whispered a number of filthy imprecations at Gloria Rabun, who was not entirely displeased.

Warlock felt soiled. Just a half a dozen hours ago he had been in the arms and legs of Laura, now he was sitting submerged in loud punk rock, his jawbones clenched with cocaine. But he knew it was part of the job. He had busted one case, maybe two: a paralyzed lover and a full motel, and in a short time he had weaseled his way into Mrs. Rabun's charmed circle of wastrels. She was admittedly regal; she somehow looked built for spending money. The cowboy artist lurched toward the toilet with his hands covering his mouth, blasting socialites and nits out of his path. Gloria summoned Warlock to her side with an imperious little pat.

"Are you a spy sent down from Traverse City by my husband?" She was smiling.

"Am I a what?" His brain spun, clutching for resources.

"Don't be silly, just truthful. My husband, Gerald, sends people down here to keep an eye on me. I usually sleep with them and send them back."

"It would be nice to sleep with you but I'm afraid I don't know your husband. Is that the first step?"

"Maybe not. And maybe you're a little too sharp for Gerald. Please excuse me."

"Not at all. I won't excuse you unless I can see you again. Let's say I'm a man on the run from a bad marriage and possible embezzlement charges. Should I face all the bad music or hightail it down to old Brazil? You tell me. Meanwhile I'm going to blow this fucking chichi pop stand." He gave her an unnecessarily familiar kiss just as the cowboy returned. Warlock was grabbed rudely by the arm. "Just leaving." He stood and waved the man to his chair which he removed at the last possible moment. He exited to a crash and screams.

At the Brazilian Court there was an envelope under the door. He waited to open it until in bed in order to savor even more intrigue. Then he remembered how hotels send up an accounting sheet of room services and tossed it aside.

He laughed at the idea of the drunk crashing to the floor. It was strange how people seemed to worship the ancient magic of the arts. The most fungoid, sallow, pimply student in a beret, given the sufficient stretch of arrogance, could convince an otherwise sensible girl to undress, to "pose" as it were, in a strange denial of mores and a craving for what might pass as immortality. Glands athwart, I am forever, the subject thinks in the dull heat of vanity. Where is sleep now. Laura in the moonlight yearns to be ambulatory but the god of the Brownian movement has stretched his loins otherwise. Could he go over there and stand on the lawn amid the sad desultory blacks in their hateful pruning and yell like a rabid Jesus "Take up thy bed and walk," walk over here, *tout de suite,* and feel this stupid heart leaking on the bedsheets with the setting moon through the window an irrevocable white rose, a visitation by the deaf and dumb Virgin Herself. Laura, let's go down to the beach and swim out too far: buoyed, no doubt, by dolphins we'll follow the white sheer of moonglitter across the water. Give me a yes or no. Let there be light, but more so, heat.

38

"Dearest Johnny," Laura wrote, "I lay here in the quiet pre-dawn hours trying to fathom your cruelty. Do you worship Satan himself? You have flung me in a short time from the highest degree of happiness to the depths of sorrow. I am so lonely. When I was at Pratt I copied down a quote from a book by Kierkegaard that was required reading in philosophy—remember when he was all the craze? 'There are occasions when it gives one a sense of infinite sadness to see a human being standing all alone in the world. Thus the other day I saw a poor girl walk all alone to church to be confirmed.' Dearest Johnny, can your evil soul comprehend this? I am that girl. Even my children are not truly mine because Bob forced me to have them. I love them but they are not mine. What happened is Bob returned from the Jai-Alai Fronton and I told him about our wonderful evening. He always makes me tell him about my little peccadilloes because it stimulates him. This time he screamed with laughter and said the only person who would fuck a crippled lady is an insurance investigator. I said no. I said you were a lovely poetic man. Bob kept saying I'll have the fucker killed and I kept saying you weren't an insurance investigator. You should know I suppose that Bob Fardel is really Roberto Fardello. Why did I marry a gangster? My family forced me into it to save their declining fortunes. Gangsters like to marry socialites, just like in *The Great Gatsby* by Fitzgerald. He said 'what was your name' and I refused until he finally held a burning cigarette near my eye. And I knew anyway you were a gentleman not an insurance investigator. So he called a connection in Detroit who has access to police records. And there you were listed as working for Dr. Rabun who owns the spa where I was injured. I wept while Bob laughed. Gloria Rabun is a neighbor of ours and a friend. It was she who suggested we sue her husband after the accident, saying he was a nasty tightwad who wouldn't let her spend her own money. Bob only wanted to have his men torch the spa. So, my dearest Johnny, I spent the night begging for your life. He made me do so many awful things but he often does that. So your life is spared, my evil darling. Did you only enter me to see if I could move? Don't answer that. I knew together we became one with the moon, if only for a moment. Today I am traveling by ambulance Lear to the Tulane Medical Center in New Orleans for my operation. If I am not cured I will kill myself. Bob agrees with this decision. So farewell, my dearest Johnny. Bob is reading this as I write. He congratulates you on your abilities but says that you must know that if you ever seek my company again he will have his henchmen chop you and your family in pieces with machetes. Despite this threat, my love, I know we will see each other again if only in heaven or hell. *Ave atque vale,* love. I still have part of you inside me. Perhaps it will grow and your baby will die with me, or live. Good-bye, Laura."

There was a childish imprint of lipstick on the bottom of the page. It wasn't the sort of letter a man wanted to get when he awoke at noon with a bad hangover. Warlock's bowels gurgled with fear, and he jumped from bed at the same time there was a knock at the door. It was an attractive young lady with an expensively wrapped present. Always a sucker for presents, he did not consider until he was on the toilet a minute later that the package might have contained high explosives. Instead there was an attractive, very dead pompano with a white rose stuck in its mouth. A joke fish? It smelled fresh but he had no cooking utensils. His thoughts flipped back and forth between Laura's letter and the dead pompano in his hands. He pulled out the rose but there was no message attached to the stem so he stuck it in a glass of water. The contemporary artist, Garth, had been helpful with the squid. Warlock misdialed twice.

"Garth. Warlock here. Johnny Lundgren down here in Florida on a frankly secret mission . . ."

"Call back later. You've caught me in midstroke." Garth began to put the receiver down until he heard a raspy yell. "My god. Please!" Warlock finally allowed the full measure of his franticness to arise to the surface. "I'll be short. What does it mean when you get a present that's a dead fish with a rose in its mouth?"

"What movie was it in? Had to be Italian."

"No. Right now. Here in my room. The present just came and I don't have a kitchenette."

"That's easy. Run for it. Drop the fish and run for it. It's an ancient Sicilian death threat. You are the dead fish and the rose is an obvious symbol of the funereal spirit in the culture of that ancient land. Did I tell you I went there last spring? Wonderful place."

"You're not pulling my leg?" Warlock's breath now came in short gasps.

"If it was me I'd fly to Houston and bribe myself onto one of those hideous space capsules. Or go to Johns Hopkins for a sex change. Just don't come here because I don't want to be involved. What in god's name did you do, fuck somebody's underage daughter?"

"A wife. She was sort of crippled. In a way."

"Wonderful. You're becoming artistic, very late in your life I might add. What I want you to do right now is call the beautiful Diana and tell her she is willed to me."

"You're not very helpful." Warlock was trying to identify a strange sensation coming over his body. It was the need to go to the toilet again: fear had shorn him of all spontaneity.

"I didn't fuck a mobster's crippled wife. You did. I'm being honest. I'm throwing the raw meat on the floor. This world's for the meat eaters, baby. They shouldn't let you charming feebs off the farm." Garth was slipping into the same gangster patois used by Dad.

"Okay. Sorry to bother you. I'll call Diana and say you're the most disgusting human I've ever known." Warlock slammed down the phone and began to pack a shoulder case. Why had he left his .38 at home? For the first time in forty-two years his life had been threatened. It was like jumping out of a comic book and landing in World War II.

A half hour later there was the prolonged hysteria of indecision at the cloverleaf of the Florida Turnpike. North or south? Warlock made a dozen turns, turnbacks, circles, pauses. Would Fardello assume he would hightail it for home, in which case he should head south? Or would Fardello assume, in that the man had complimented Warlock's abilities, that he would go south? There was virtually no east what with the Atlantic, and west on the map held Sarasota, the name of which didn't have enough masculine consonants to sound safe. He must not lead these immigrant fiends back to Michigan. Hadn't Laura said she had begged for his life, performing unnameable acts on Bob? Could he put total stock in the whimsical Garth, an art type who had made frequent passes at Diana in defiance of friendship and trust? Garth's gimcrack southern elegance concealed Irish blood, not the most trustworthy people in conversation, where any fib could be told in favor of a turn of phrase. The image of swart types dressed like Marlon Brando in *Guys and Dolls* finally turned him south. There was the cowering but stately Diana advanced on by men with machetes. Rape wasn't out of the question. He desperately needed the solace of her company but he knew he must give up his safety for her own.

It took seven hours and two speeding tickets to reach Key West. His extreme nervousness had forced several meal and drink stops. There was that well known tradition of the "last meal" afforded the condemned man, and he tried to be inventive in his menu studies, somewhat in the manner of one who is asked what book or woman one would take to a desert island? The Bible and Monica Vitti, Shakespeare and Lauren Hutton, Toynbee and Jessica Lange, *Garp* and Gilda Radner, *Pat the Bunny* and Brooke Shields?

By early evening he had arrived at the shrimp docks in Key West with a full belly and heavy heart. In his bookish casing of the hometown of Rabun's son he had noted the substantial shrimp fleet that used Key West as home port. He would abandon the BMW and sign on as a burly deckhand for the fabled shrimping grounds off Guatemala. He did not particularly favor this lowest of crustaceans as table fare but there was an image of warm seas, Caribbean ports laden with rum and octoroons, tattoos, and so on. He walked out on the windy dock and smelled the deep, terrible smell of the ill-kept boats. Fear had exhausted him and the fierce wind in the riggings brought back memories of near fatal seasickness on the Great Lakes.

39

Those people of northern climes should be forewarned that the tropics are not the best place to undergo a depression; much is made of that old bugaboo of stress these days, and what might cause greater stress than the fact that you and your loved ones will be hacked in pieces by long knives, intended to beat a peaceful pathway through the jungle? The machete, heraldic weapon of the current dope war that rages through Florida; a war, unseen by tourists, of muffled weapons, gurgles, slamming car doors, the putt of silencers, of vast sums of money being laundered in the presidential chambers of banks while your grandma withdraws her Christmas savings out front. Yes, Warlock was only gradually mindful of his birthday two days hence, and the oncoming folly of Christmas. Death and the Christmas season, the creeping sun-blasted rot of the tropics, the forced gaiety of Key West; had Warlock been the least bit suicidal the ensuing week would have finished him. It was a time of testing that he would remember with clenched fists even on his deathbed.

After that first evening at the shrimp docks, when the foul

smell of deliquescing crustaceans signaled a change in plans, liquor led him into a manic rage, and more liquor led him into a greater manic rage. He took grandiose accommodations at the Pier House, forgetting in a liquor haze that he should be becoming less visible. He had a grandiose French meal, forgetting in a liquor haze that his tummy was already full. He went to a club with a view of the harbor, having secured the name of this hot spot from a waitress, and had a grandiose number of drinks, and some grandiose lines of cocaine with the waitress when she showed up to trim her grandiose pigeon. She went to his quarters with him, then left with the toot he had purchased while he was kneeling, elbows on the toilet bowl, and ridding himself of the rainbow colors of the evening. The plus factor in his behavior is that it could not immediately be construed as suicidal, except by a psychiatrist.

But even this deluge of mind destroyers did not give Warlock a full night's sleep; he was up early and shaking, composing a list that would act as a drawstring of order. After an uneaten breakfast and the purchase of some stomach soothers he arranged to have the tan rental BMW painted gray by some merry Cubans at a bump shop on Ann Street. He bought a large valise of assorted used clothes, remembering J. Kirk Barefoot's admonition not to use disguises unless you're skillful. He got a close cropped Navy-style haircut and decided to grow a mustache. He bought a nearly indelible false tattoo at a novelty shop; a tattoo, a little smeared in application, that showed a cobra and panther poised for mortal combat. In a compact rental he drove to the Searstown Plaza for the first of ten sessions in a suntan parlor. He stopped barely short of a gold ring for his ear. He ate an extra large, starchy Cuban meal. He went to bed at eight in the evening (in a house trailer he had rented out on Stock Island) after watching a pleasantly distracting half hour of the Muppets.

He nearly slept through his next tanning appointment, though it proved especially boring without the excitement of coffee in his gullet. Somehow he had slept fourteen hours and Warlock felt the dull, chastened humility of the POW, which exactly fitted his new appearance. He was momentarily appalled by the stark weirdo in the tanning parlor mirror—the faded old clothes, and criminal mien—until he recognized himself. Had he gone too far, he wondered? But what was too far when you were saving your life? Why had the man at the desk at the tanning parlor called him "darling"? He reached Diana at the nurse's lounge from a pay phone on A1A. Why had someone peed on the floor of the phone booth?

"Johnny. How are you, lover? Getting any sun?"

"A little. It's been tough down here but I'm doing real well."

"Nothing dangerous? Promise me you won't do anything silly and dangerous."

"I promise, baby." His tear ducts swelled with a mad urge to spill the beans about his current peril.

"Our first newsletter came out. It's fabulous. Can I send it or will you be home pretty soon?"

"I'm in Sarasota right now." Perhaps Fardello was tapping his home phone, he thought quickly. "There's a chance you might have to come down for Christmas. I'm real busy."

"Gee, I don't know. I promised Mom. We'll see. I got to run to surgery. I miss you. You're supposed to call Rabun, Feingold, and your dad. Your dad is quite the flirt on the phone. And Garth called with the usual filth but he said he had talked to you."

When he left the phone booth two gay men waved a greeting and Warlock felt a blush rise slowly to his still-pallid face. What was the deal, he wondered? He didn't want to make any more phone calls in a booth that smelled like pee-pee. He forgave Diana for the fact that her concern could not possibly match the degree of his trepidation. It might just be time to check on the two addresses he had for Rabun's son. The disguise was gradually allowing his inherent strength to regather itself, a strength that had carried him through lesser crises, and now seemed to be mustering itself for the big one.

The compact car had a comforting overheated quality to it. Danger, secrecy, stealth, were all conducive to sweat. He would ask Dad to run an exhaustive check on Roberto Fardello. As frightened as he had been, Warlock's stomach and shoulders now tightened in reaction. A certain Palm Beach Sicilian ganglord, kingpin, bully, wife-beater, Mafia don, might just have bitten off a little more than he could chew. I'm a tad tougher than pasta, Warlock thought.

There was a shifty piece of vertigo in his stomach when he discovered that neither of the addresses he had been given for Rabun's son existed. His mind wandered into the idea behind "a wild goose chase"; even tame geese were nearly impossible to catch unless strictly confined. He went into what looked like a working class bar for his first drink in thirty-six hours, a time span that proved his limited good sense. It was just that self-criticism sometimes crippled a man.

The bar was blindingly dark and he stood still for a full minute to avoid tripping. There was a curious sense of danger, as if he was on the verge of being sucker-punched. There was an odd sprinkling of hippies, fishing guides and layabouts. Warlock returned the bearded bartender's rude stare.

"I'd like some sort of strange drink of the tropics."

"We'd prefer if you would drink at a bar with your own kind, sir."

"What's my kind for god's sake?" Warlock had sat down before the full import of the statement had hit him. Everyone was staring at him with a kind of science fiction intensity.

"He's saying that down here heterosexuals and homosexuals don't make a habit of drinking together," a big fat man said.

"Well, I'm sorry." Warlock was puzzled by everyone's appearance. They certainly didn't look gay. "Why don't you hang out a sign saying this is a gay bar?" There was a roar of laughter. Now the truth was beginning to hit him like a shit monsoon. He laid out a hundred dollar bill to cover the drink that had not yet appeared. The bartender still stood there with arms folded as the laughter died. "Look, Tonto"—Warlock's voice was quaking with injustice—"If you're calling me a queer I'm going to rip that fucking mop off your face. You got a ten count to get me a drink. Ten-nine-eight . . ."

"Maybe he ain't a queer," the fat man said. "I'll buy him a drink."

"Coming up," the bartender said. "Where are you from?"

"Michigan," Warlock said. There was more laughter. His hand shook as it tried to enclose the glass. He had entered an insane asylum, forgetting that all bars are essentially insane asylums.

"You don't understand that you're all dressed up like a homo with that short haircut, phony tattoo, man-tan, little mustache, jeans and old work shirt? That's the problem," the fat man said.

"What about you?" The fat man had a short haircut.

"Obese, diabetic fishing guides with no money who have been married seven times are rarely cocksuckers."

The cocktail hour wore on, as they say. After a half dozen piña coladas Warlock made an impassioned plea for world sexual understanding which was met with boos. It seems the gays were taking over the town, aided by left-wing realtors; the poor locals were being driven from their homes as if a cruel, invading army were entering the city. Warlock had been nominally involved in the civil rights movement and began to see gays as blacks in the early sixties.

"What about gay blacks?" he asked, apropos of nothing, after the conversation had turned to fishing and weather. No one answered.

40

Always one to make the best of a thoroughly bad situation, Warlock concluded that his inadvertent disguise might help him break through the homosexual underground, or overground, as it appeared to be in Key West where these people cavorted in public at will. The Sunday school lesson of Sodom and Gomorrah came to mind but he had forgotten the conclusion other than a woman had been turned into a pillar of salt. His getup, therefore, assumed the virtue of being in the line of duty: Rabun's son was gay and might very well be held captive in some sort of gay hideout. The son's request for a quarter of a million dollars to start a gay restaurant might be a concealed ransom plea. These people were feminine, frivolous, inventive; according to Garth, he had been thwarted in the art world by the gay art Mafia. Warlock had tended to take Garth's complaint *cum grano salis,* principally because the man's art seemed to be a dull, faddish sham compared to that of the great Gauguin.

All these thoughts—rather, these questionable assumptions —whirred in his mind on the dawn of his forty-third birthday.

Dawn was not his favorite time by any means but Bib, the fat man from the cocktail lounge, had promised him a boat ride. The previous, uneventful day had led him to a huge marina he had discovered just down the road from his dreary trailer. The whole trailer camp was littered with vicious guard dogs on short chains; at least the economically defeated could own big mean dogs. This served to make him sentimental and lonely for old Hudley. The tropics had tended to defeat his naturally sentimental disposition: gravel roads, barn swallows, baby mice, the Save the Children ads on TV, all swept him away into a state where his throat would constrict, and which could only be relieved by a long sigh. Anyway, he had gone to the marina and remet Bib, who sat with a group of other idle fishing guides drinking beer and eating smoked fish. Bib had embarrassingly explained to the guides that Warlock wasn't a "homo," but an undercover man from Michigan. The sixth piña colada had evidently made Warlock indiscreet. But the information made the guides very respectful, and after a few beers Warlock regaled them with tailing tactics cribbed from J. Kirk Barefoot.

"A few years ago I was tracking the blond wife of a very prominent auto executive in Detroit. You'd all recognize the name, though I'm not at liberty to divulge it. It was a tough divorce case with a lot of property on the line. The marriage was kaput and the executive had fallen in love with his old high school sweetheart but his young current wife wouldn't let him go. He knew she was playing around, in fact, it's fair to say she was a nympho."

Warlock was a wise enough student of human nature to know that the word *nympho* had captured the audience. "Anyway, I tailed her for a month using a van rig with a periscope capable of taking pictures in the air vent on top. I tailed her to many a love nest but couldn't chance pictures through any windows because she was always accompanied by two Doberman pinschers. One fine June day I followed her into the country north of Detroit and there on an old gravel road, through a spotting scope, I saw her meet a very big, very black Detroit Lion football player whose name you would recognize. The adulterous couple slipped off into the woods with a blanket and picnic basket with the guard dogs. You should all know I'm from northern Michigan and spend a lot of time hunting. I circled the couple downwind to avoid the dogs picking up my scent. I was moving through the woods like a fucking Indian when I heard a noise. I raised my binoculars to which a small camera is attached. There they were in a position too embarrassing to describe. . . ."

"Oh for god's sake tell us," Bib howled.

"Up north they call it dog-style." There was much muttering, swearing, amazement at the perfidy of women. "Well, I got my pictures in a hurry but then my luck changed. The wind switched and the dogs picked up my scent. They were between me and my car a quarter mile away. I hightailed it in the other direction. I could see the Detroit River in the distance when the dogs closed in, and I had to shoot them both. I ran through the yard of a vacant cabin and out onto a dock. There was a rowboat but it was locked up tight with a chain. I saw the football player coming around the cabin in his undershorts at a dead run, looking a lot bigger than Marion Motley, Jimmy Brown, Earl Campbell, all put together. I coolly put my exposed film in a small canister and stuck the canister in my mouth. I dove in the river and swam for Canada some two miles distant. Lucky for me I won my letter in swimming at Michigan State. I heard him yelling from the dock but I had won the day. I called the auto executive from the other side and he sent a man to pick me up. I had a photographic studio blow the pictures up to poster size. When the wife and her ace lawyer, Feingold, were confronted with the photos they shit in their pants. End of story."

"I would have shot the nigger on the dock," one of the guides said with a southern drawl. There was a chorus of head shaking assent.

"I'm a professional. I wasn't mad at the black for screwing a beautiful blonde who put him up to it. If I had been the husband I might have gotten away with murder legally. And the guy was a great ballplayer. Don't forget the Detroit Lions need all the help they can get."

"I sure would like to see those pictures," said a young dockhand. "They can't swim good because of their muscles."

"I had one up on the wall of my den but my wife made me take it down." Warlock felt a bit henpecked after adding that detail. Hadn't he burned all of his pornography? Why couldn't he keep this imaginary photo in the imaginary den decorated with shelves of imaginary crime classics, awards, photos, the imaginary paraphernalia of his dark profession?

A little later he went to the cocktail lounge with Bib, and they planned his birthday boat trip. Then he remembered the name Feingold from the story and excused himself for a call.

"Look, the doctor is trying to make contact. Gloria Rabun sent an abusive letter saying that at least his latest spy was charming."

"It's a red herring. She's fishing. I've convinced her otherwise. In fact, we're nearly intimate. Relay that message because I don't have time for simpleminded phone calls. I have reason to suspect I'm being followed by the Mafia."

"Jesus! Be careful. You're not having delusions, are you?"

"Do you call a machete wound on the shoulder a delusion?"

"I guess not. Are you getting much?"

"Too much. I put it on the shelf every few days to let it heal. Even a dick needs a vacation."

"You lucky dog," Feingold sighed.

The birthday boat trip turned out to be more than a little frightening. The morning weather was calm and exhilarating but Bib's notion of the proper speed was full throttle on his overpowered skiff. They traveled some forty miles west, out past the Marquesas, where they watched a large tug combing the bottom for buried treasure. A breeze picked up from the northeast and they jumped their lunch hour ahead from noon to ten. They went through a half case of beer and a twenty piece bucket of commercially fried chicken Bib had bought the evening before. Mashed potatoes and gravy accompanied the bucket but they were cold and congealed from a night in the refrigerator.

"This gravy's no fucking good," Bib said, making a gelatinous snowball out of the gravy and throwing it at a pelican. The pelicans also rejected the coleslaw, rolls, mashed potatoes, and chicken bones. "I've brought you here for a reason," Bib said, wiping his mouth with an oily rag. "An ancient gold coin from the wreck these guys are diving on. Your little woman will just cream her drawers under the Christmas tree when you spring this one on her. The coin is dated and has a certificate of authenticity from authorities. It's worth a grand but I'll let you have it for eight hundred because I like you. Why else would I be burning up expensive gas in the middle of the goddamn ocean if I didn't like you?"

Warlock bought the questionable coin after eliciting a promise that they would return immediately to Key West. He had to throw in an extra hundred to have the coin mounted and a gold chain attached. By then the northeaster had increased to the point that he was struggling to keep the chicken down. Why was the food of Key West backing up on him? He held on with prayer during the long, slamming, jarring ride back to town.

At the marina there was a crazed Russian urge to kiss the greasy boards of the dock. Through the sting of the dried salt spray around his eyes he saw a young guide spraying down his boat at the next slip. Warlock borrowed the hose to rinse his face. The sign of the neighboring boat read THE LOON— CAPT. TED RABUN. Oh my god. He returned the hose with a sly smile.

"Like to book you. I've heard about you."

"Got a free day on Saturday. You got tackle?"

"No. I'll be here at eight. You want a deposit?" The young man shook his head. Warlock's heart swelled temporarily, but then he thought, could there be two Ted Rabuns? Not likely, but he didn't want to chance another day on the high seas.

41

Some birthday, he thought, back at the trailer, and still seasick enough to be unable to lie down. Some fucking lonely birthday. Except for the three years in the Air Force, Warlock had always received the meal of his choice on his birthday. No presents. No nothing. After the fried chicken hysteria he wasn't hungry but the day of his birth was only half over. And that jerk Fardello was forcing him to live in a trashy mobile home when he should be in a suite at the Pier House where beautiful women sunbathed topless. Diana wouldn't be singing him her lilting version of the old favorite, "Happy Birthday." And more important, Diana always proffered the unusual gift of letting his sexual imagination run playfully on this special day. The only limitation was pain, which neither of them enjoyed. He chuckled at the memory of the previous year when at his insistence she had tied him to the bed and put him through Amazonian sex tortures. Then, at the stroke of midnight, she had declared the game over, saying that Gretchen needed to talk to her. He had shouted himself hoarse as she dressed and walked out. He heard the car start and Hudley had come in and barked at him for private reasons. She was quite the jokester, driving around the block before her return and more unfettered fun.

The memory was giving him a hardon aided by a thirteen year old girl sunbathing on a patch of lawn next to the neighboring trailer. She couldn't be any older than that but he escalated his notion of her age to make his fantasy legal. He had been in Key West four or five days and didn't know any girls, though there was a dim, alcohol clouded memory of the first night's waitress. Debby? Donna? Doris? Shit. Now the girl got on her hands and knees to smooth her blanket, aiming a round little hinder straight at his window. He released his hardon out into the foetid air of the trailer. Why not? Pants dropped to ankles. Unluckily, orgasm caused a momentary dizziness and he grabbed the drapes to avoid falling. The drapes didn't hold and he fell backwards to the floor in an onanistic mess of drapes and jism. His head narrowly missed a possibly fatal blow from the coffee table. A lesser man could become depressed, he thought, trying to find something positive in the situation.

It was oddly comfortable on the floor, giving him a new perception of the trailer: there were clots of dried gum wads and boogers on the underside of the coffee table, and the name "Frank" scrawled in red crayon. Or Crayola? Was Frank the messy little gum chewing villain? Had the nymphet heard the crash and been alarmed? The bottom of the kitchen table was also a mess, a soiled minimalist painting. No wonder little children behave badly what with this grim view of their world, a world of dog bellies and dust curls, of bunioned feet and pant cuffs, the darkness up Daddy's robe and Mommy's dress. He remembered the garters cutting into his aunt's thighs. Why had he been stupid enough to try to hypnotize this aunt when he was fifteen? He had ordered the hypnotism book from an ad in *True* magazine for five bucks, which represented two weeks' profit from a paper route. All he got was a slap in the face when he touched her supposedly sedated thigh. Who wants to be young again when that sort of thing happens? So yummy through the bathroom keyhole, the nascent hormonal buzz turning into a jet roar. She was napping in a plaid skirt with Sunday comics spread across her face. Joe Palooka rose and fell to her steady breathing. She coughed and he jumped backward like a cat. Panties pulled up her bum, an effect revered in photos. You are in ancient Kashmir . . . in the golden temple of Shalazar . . . I am the caliph, your lover, the most handsome man in the world etc. I still remember the unsuccessful hypno-lingo. Days later she winked. Doze.

After a wondrous nap, troubled in its last stage by horses running around under the ground and Diana in the back of a pickup with a cowboy, he drove down to the bump shop to retrieve his BMW. He gave a strolling hippie twenty bucks to follow him out to the airport with the rental compact. Unfortunately the hippie never arrived at the car rental office. After an hour the police came to take Warlock's statement.

"You're liable!" shrieked the rental agent for the fiftieth time, and now for the benefit of the police.

"I don't care," was Warlock's standard reply.

"You irresponsible faggot! You fucking queer!"

The irresponsible statement got the car rental agent picked up by the tie and belt, and shaken senseless. The police made no effort to interfere. Warlock had already slipped them his identification papers. He swore out a complaint against the agent for foul language in a public place, then drove off with a light heart. A simple nickel-and-dime car theft wasn't going to spoil his birthday.

Warlock drove slowly past Captain Ted Rabun's house, the address gotten, in a smart move, out of the phone book. A pretty young woman sat on the porch dandling an infant. Ruse or wife? Great sums of money were the obvious impulse behind most of the deceit on earth. What better way to cover up your depravity than by becoming a fishing guide? You had to check out all of the sides of the coin, which were two in number. Or facets of the diamond face of reality. When reality whirled it became a basketball with no sides, he decided, when the narrow streets became confusing and he ended up driving by Captain Ted's house the second time. Now the wife or ruse wasn't on the front porch. Neither was the baby. They must have gone inside, he thought; hopefully she didn't sense that the man in the expensive car wasn't exactly a friend of the family. Diana and the cowboy flitted through his mind like dream tatters. How did dreams make up people that didn't exist? There weren't any cowboys in Michigan and Diana had never really left his company on their Wyoming trip. Guys who wrote letters to *Penthouse* frequently described themselves as hiding in closets and watching their wives gleefully receive members of awesome proportions, if the writers could be believed. The owners of the disproportionate organs were usually old army buddies named Bill or Bob. There were a number of variations on this inscrutable theme. Thank god I'm normal, he thought.

He drove down to the Pier House for a drink on the deck, but the afternoon light was waning and there was only a single topless sunbather left on the narrow beach. One of her teats, interestingly enough, was larger than the other. A number of polyester dodos were drinking on the deck and pretending not to look at the hapless woman. Warlock felt poignant despair about the whole sexual question until he discovered the waitress of his first night in town passing by with a tray of drinks.

"It can't be you!" She was amazed at his undercover guise.

"You might say it's me. There's a reason behind everything. It's my birthday, how about a gourmet French dinner?"

"If you're after your cocaine I lost it." She was a wary lass.

"Cocaine, schmocaine. There's more where that came from, baby." He was learning that this drug was the prime pussy bait of the age.

His heart felt a speculative soar as he showered and dressed. A lonely birthday had to be an exception to the whole fidelity rap. As a not totally self-acknowledged Calvinist he was a master at exceptions. Life was a ladder on which some of the rungs were icy, slippery, precarious; one hedged a bit sexually, or in terms of business ethics, but that didn't mean you had fallen to the primordial, bestial foot of the ladder. You didn't have the easy out of Catholic penance, guppy munchers as Dad called them, but you had the Siamese Twins of Grace and Predestination on your side.

The dinner was pretty good and since it was his birthday, he did not puzzle long over the three desirable entrées: duck bigarade, duck Montmorency, lobster crêpes. He ordered all three, along with Montrachet and a Chambertin. This served to make the management suspect that he might be a restaurant critic, a trick taught Warlock by the artist and trencherman, Garth. You paid the bill, but the service and food tended to be first rate. Lucette, the waitress date, nibbled like a big bunny at her plate of poached vegetables, though she hit the wine pretty hard. Aurora came to mind. Was he attracted in some strange way to vegetarian women, or they to him? Would they finally suffer the mental problems of protein starvation, or was this a superior life instinct?

They went to her humble apartment, decorated in part by the same Manolete poster of yore, a coincidence he found charming. She sold him two grams of Peruvian rock, a mysterious term of the drug trade. He did a great deal of it to overcome the soporific effects of the meal, and was soon buzzing like a defective toaster. Lucette, it turned out, was a serious voice student "just waitressing for the bucks." At his insistence she sang, accompanying herself with a guitar. Her operatic voice was embarrassing when singing popular tunes. Only a foot away on the couch she sang muddled lines of "I Believe," "He Got da Whole Wurl in His Hand" (her pronunciation) and "White Rabbit." He felt a fine spray of operatic spittle. Would this coke crazed cunt never stop? She finally did. They stripped following a subtle eye signal but then his dick wouldn't work, an aftereffect of the drug he remembered from Aurora. They did hours of "other stuff" as Lucette called it. She was a gymnast who reminded him of Elsa Lanchester in *Bride of Frankenstein*. By dawn he finally got a genuine boner and covered her sleeping body with desperation.

42

Twenty-four hours later Warlock was skipping across the northwest channel with Captain Ted Rabun at dawn, headed for the vast tidal flats off Cottrell Key. It had taken a full twenty-four hours to begin to recover from the brain-curdling mud bath with Lucette. What a relief pure nature was, especially when the water of the flats was shallow and there was no chance of drowning. Lucette's soprano occasionally still trilled in his ears in hideous flashbacks, harkening back to the droll fifties when his faculty advisor and chums would sing folk songs —"dicka dicka derry dum dum doodoo"—that sort of thing. The Irish were given to this sort of nonsense, which cost them a lot of tourist dollars, Warlock thought.

Captain Ted pulled back on the throttle and eased the boat up into even shallower water. Their prey would be the wily permit; a picture of the fish at the marina tackle shop looked uncomfortably like the gift pompano in Palm Beach. He thought again of the immense messiness in nature, what with the thousands of kinds of fish, bugs, birds, as if God hadn't been able to put two and two together. Warlock turned to find

Captain Ted Rabun leveling a pistol at him, right smack dab in the middle.

"Jeezo-peezo! What's the deal?" His breath exploded.

"I've got you where I want you. Get out of the boat."

He fired a shot into the water to emphasize his seriousness.

"Okay, okay. Don't get excited." Warlock eased himself over the gunwhale, sinking to mid-thigh in the water and the grassy marl of the bottom.

"Toss me your billfold." When Warlock paused, Rabun fired another bullet near his left knee. "Make it snappy."

Captain Ted sorted through the contents of the wallet in a jiffy. Warlock felt a strong tickling sensation deep in his bowels. What on earth could be happening; was the son a less benign lunatic than his father?

"Could you please explain your actions?" Warlock sensed that a shark of fatal proportions was in the vicinity.

"I knew it!" Ted Rabun was looking at a driver's license. "I knew it. My mother said you drove a tan BMW but you had a compact at the marina. Then my wife said a gray BMW passed our house twice. Bib told me you were an undercover man from Michigan but you didn't fit Gloria's description. So you pull up in that car and I look closely and think, it's got to be you. Have a nice walk. Wait for a passing boat because the ship channel is full of big sharks." Rabun started the motor.

"Please!" Warlock's legs weakened to the point that he sat down in the water; it was warm and vaguely comforting, an amniotic fluid that would serve as a liquid shroud. "My god man, are you a savage?"

"No. I'm a fishing guide and you're just another shit-faced spy my father sent down. Did he say I was a heroin addict?" Rabun throttled down to hear the answer; Gloria had said that this was by far the least crummy spy of the last decade.

"No, that's not what he said." Warlock felt his inventiveness slip gears. He had read that a woman should try to start a dialogue with her rapist. What's your major and your favorite color? Maybe, for once, honesty really was the best policy. Rabun's boat was now fifty feet away, drifting with a slow outmoving tide. "He said you were a homo and trying to con two hundred and fifty grand out of him to start a gay restaurant. I speculated that you might be being blackmailed, you know, say by gay criminals or something."

"Oh my god!" Captain Ted Rabun gave a comforting laugh. "Mom said you were goofy. Look at that fucking stupid disguise." The boat was drifting farther away and their voices rose to the occasion.

"I had to change my appearance. I had a brief affair with a crippled friend of your mother's, Laura Fardel. Her husband, the mobster Roberto Fardello, threatened my life. I raced down here and went underground. I thought I may as well check you out. It's just my job." Warlock now was shouting at the distant boat which was being sucked toward the channel in the tidal swirl.

Captain Ted was jumping around his boat screaming with helpless laughter. He was nearly out of earshot before he started up the engine and idled closer. Warlock saw a group of fins in the distance and made a vain attempt to run for it. "Shark," he screamed. Rabun drew closer.

"Those are tailing permit." He was still giggling. "They're feeding on crustaceans on the bottom and that makes their tails rise. Come aboard."

"Thanks." Warlock heaved himself into the boat. He had seen *Jaws* and his heart was racing like a Big Ben version of a stopwatch.

"Bob Fardel went to Yale Drama. He and Laura have this

thing for what they call living drama. She's very big Louisiana oil money. She had an extremely mild back injury at Dad's spa and Gloria suggested they make it hot for him. So Laura and Bob with their living drama bit see another fine opportunity." Captain Ted kept interrupting himself with laughter. He drew two cans of beer from the cooler and tossed one to Warlock.

"I don't get it." He was so glad to be back in the boat that he couldn't quite digest the information.

"When I was sixteen Bob and Laura decided I was the young love scenario and you can imagine what happened. Bob directs the whole shot. Gloria told me on the phone about the cripple scenario. Laura's been luring guys off the beach while Bob's in the upstairs bedroom directing operations with hand signals, binoculars and video camera." Captain Ted spit out beer in another gale of laughter.

"It just can't be so. It can't be." Warlock's vertigo was too deep for simple dizziness; it was a chill, numbing sensation that covered his entire body, three quarters of which was wet. He picked an infant shrimp off his shoe. Little lamb, who made thee?

"You might like to know the quarter million represents two years of my trust that started two years ago when I was twenty-one. Dad is crazy. He's been crazy for thirteen years since we got kicked out of Cincinnati where I grew up. Mother had all the dough and she marries this genius medical researcher, my dad. Everything was fine until I was about ten. Mom sends Dad off to this super fat clinic where he loses well over a hundred pounds. He used to be jolly and wonderful but within a few months he becomes a monster. We had this summer place near Traverse City and we had to move there when the authorities in Cincinnati decided Dad was too hot to handle.

He got caught in bed with these teen-agers he had fed a lot of dope to. Mom's family had the power to protect him for about a year. They sent him to Menninger's and a few other places. He came back to his senses enough to keep out of jail. During all the good years when he was an inventor he was also a financial genius and he got control of about half of Mom's money and all of my trust. Now he won't give me a dime. In a way I feel bad for him and in a way I hate him when I remember the perverted things he did to Mom. Christ, he can't even get into Palm Beach anymore. There was an expensive cover-up a few years back when he tried some weird sexual invention on an underage girl and she was injured, though not seriously."

Warlock couldn't raise his voice past a mumble. He watched a group of alarmed cormorants fly off as the boat drifted toward them, shitting at the last moment to lighten themselves for flight. He was not about to draw conclusions from cormorants or Captain Ted Rabun; it was all too dreary for words. There was a yearning for his special pillow. "I want to go home," he said bleakly. It would be soothing to cook Diana dinner and prepare a little cheese on toast for Hudley.

The next morning Captain Ted and Warlock were speeding at dawn in a gray BMW toward Palm Beach. Even more shocking water had gone over the dam, so shocking that Warlock sat in the passenger's seat with clenched jaws while Ted put the car through its paces. In a twenty-four hour baptism of fire he had experienced the soaring bitterness of sophistication, the bitter fruit of comprehending a large portion of reality. Captain Ted had taken this broken waif home and fed him a fine Hunanese meal (cold chicken salad with noodles and cucumber slices, ginger shrimp, hot and sour fish), and his lovely wife had let Warlock rock their colicky infant to sleep, singing "Bobby Shafto's gone to sea, a silver buckle on his knee, he'll come back and marry me, pretty Bobby Shafto." He hadn't been able to locate Diana on the phone. He called his dad to run an exhaustive make on Dr. Rabun. He called Clete because he somehow wanted to talk to Hudley, which wasn't possible. Clete said it was urgent that he call Patty, she of the bowling alley parking lot blowjob. Promiscuity was somewhat limited in Traverse City and Clete was a roamer, running into Patty at the selfsame bowling alley. Warlock contacted Patty and, after some arch inanities, was informed that her mother was Dr. Rabun's cleaning woman, and this selfsame Rabun was having a long-standing affair with Warlock's wife, Diana. Patty chortled maniacally until Warlock hung up with dry sobs shooting convulsively through his body. Dad called in while Ted and Warlock were conceiving a plan to turn the tables.

"Johnny? Your so-called employer is the biggest pervert in the country. I would not trust a Holstein in his vicinity. He should be destroyed like a rabid dog but all these airhead liberals . . ." Warlock hung up on Dad. Hate swelled in his heart.

43

Winter slept its sleep. Warlock's spirit went under the ground with the tubers, roots, the stones that have never seen daylight and never will. In fact, his spirit stayed below any conceivable room temperature. April came, the piper at the gates of dawn. Fog rose from the melting drifts. Fox tracks spread. He cast a cold eye with a disarming friendliness. Certainly Diana and Rabun did not suspect the trap being set. He only read children's books to keep his mind cruel and simple. His mind slipped back into prehistory, enacting out of racial memory the true relationship between hunted and hunter, how the predator husbands his prey. It was not that he was a leopard playing with mating mice. He had learned, in defiance of John Calvin, that life did not usually offer up any sweetmeats of vindication, but that life's little specialties were blurred peripheries, out of focus elongated moments, shrill nights where one slept on piles of cold, dreamless coal, or fell down uncapped oil wells, dreams of funerals and headless roosters. He flew to New York and buried himself in expense account decadence like a soprano cuckoo. He returned and hiked in circles in melting snowdrifts.

He cleaned his shotgun over and over. He became lost in an April storm and was chased by a low flying cloud the size of a Greyhound bus. To say that Warlock was getting ready to make his move would be a ludicrous euphemism: he was intractable, foreordained, predestined, implacable as an ICBM sent earthwards from a galactic platform; the lever has already been pulled, the red button pushed. In a way Warlock was better than an ICBM; he was a man with a heart and brain full of hatred and he could hit a moving target. It was only a matter of time.

When Ted and Warlock had reached Palm Beach that grim but sunny mid-December day, they'd made Gloria cancel a tennis date, a luncheon, a hair appointment, a massage, a cocktail party, a dinner, a ball at the Seminole Club and a postball party at the Bath and Tennis Club. They locked themselves in Gloria's den, unplugged the phone and had a long mixture of a skull session and war party, with a coffee table strewn with the paper intricacies of Ted and Gloria's ravaged portfolios and forged trust papers. The total swindle amounted to a little over three million. Warlock drew up an airtight performance contract entitling him to a ten percent recovery fee, plus expenses. Like nearly all rich people they were not stupid and tried to nitpick the percentage downward.

"He's sixty-eight," Warlock said. "He could die any moment from the excitement of fucking my wife. Then you'd lose the whole three mil. I've seen the will." The last was a fib; rather, an outright lie.

"Well, maybe my lawyers should be here. . . ." Gloria wrung her hands in doubt.

"Let's sleep on it," Ted said in a lame waffle.

"Fuck you, you dummies!" Warlock kicked over the coffee table. "You made your feeb bed, die in it." He strode toward the door; they followed at a dead run with Gloria rubbing her bird's nest against his hip bone. He looked down at the pendulous amethyst between her breasts. Ted had a strong grip on his elbow.

"We'll sign, Mom, it's our only shot. I have doubts that he'll bring it off but it's our only chance."

They signed, then drank a few bottles of prime bubbly. Gloria's fey friend, the decorator and nightclub owner, came over and cooked them an overlight dinner of truffled omelettes, and an asparagus mousse with poached eggs buried mysteriously in the middle. Warlock was still hungry until the gay blade produced a Bon Vivant soup can with a false bottom, containing the white powder that Warlock had previously met head-on with mixed results. Palm Beach was not the town that catered to impoliteness, so he allowed his name to be written in the stuff on a black mirror. The man began with a "Hock" of Hockney.

"No. It's Warlock. Write Warlock." He snorted it through to the "l" before the substance began falling out of his nose.

"Bravo!" they all yelled, except Captain Ted who thought drugs an inimical attack on good sense. He kissed Gloria goodbye and caught a cab for a charter back to Key West.

It was a night not to be forgotten. She held him through his fits of weeping, fits of dread and paranoia, fits of the self-contempt every cuckold feels—the "aren't I enough" school of self-flagellation with berserk anger hanging in the background, just over the lip of consciousness. Her payoff came near dawn when they threw each other the sort of sorrow-drowning fuck that opens new horizons—in this case, a rendezvous in London in May.

"Why are you so wonderful?" he asked drowsily.

"Tennis, my masseur, plastic surgery, swimming and a lot of practice," she said frankly.

To be truthful, as shot through with chicanery and deceit as she was, Warlock did not, on a subliminal level, want to lose Diana. As March waned she became merry as a lark over the approaching spring. He had persuaded her that his deep depression was a result of being strafed by some Cuban thugs with Uzi machine guns. Only his ability to swim great lengths underwater had saved his skin. When she returned from work, Warlock had a not totally pleasant tendency to try to rub her article for signs of telltale dampness. But then jealousy, after self-pity, is the most destructive human emotion.

It was Dad, quite naturally, who set the trap that sprung its tungsten jaws quite neatly over Rabun's scrawny neck. Warlock flew to Minneapolis and Dad met him at the Republic gate with his dumpy second wife. Warlock, continuing his role as the forlorn waif, had fallen into his father's arms, aided, in his sentimental overdrive, by a long boozy layover at O'Hare.

"Jesus! Let go. Everyone will think we're homingtons. What shitheel gave you that haircut?"

The fact of the matter was that on his return in December only Diana had appreciated his scuffy haircut, and that was for the peculiar effect his soft, short hair had on her upper thighs.

"Are you pretending I'm someone else?" he had asked with a searing pang in his heart.

"No, not really. It just feels different. Everyone needs something different." She was hoisting herself on her own petard!

"I'm not enough?" He buried his face in the pillow, almost afraid to hear.

"I said something different, goofy. Not someone. Your hair feels like my first boyfriend, you know, back in the ninth grade."

"Did you do you know what with him?"

"Of course not. We were both Methodists He had this giant thing and I'd rub it once a week with a lot of tissues in my hand." Diana began laughing hysterically. He didn't get the joke.

Over an inedible mess of Myrna's pork paprikash at Dad's condo the plan was made. After a few swift phone calls much of the blame, other than Rabun's, was affixed on the Detroit law firm. After determining Warlock's solvency, Dad called an ace private dick in Detroit, a former employee of both the FBI and the IRS who charged five hundred bucks a day plus expenses. That matter immediately solved, Dad railed on about the ineptitude of the Minnesota Vikings until he noticed tears forming in his son's eyes.

"So what's the matter?"

"Diana's been running around."

"Big fucking deal. So write your congressman. If you got proof, tell her to stop. She's too good a lady to divorce."

"You mean it?"

"Are you kidding? Any man would give his eyetooth or thumbs for a shot at her drawers. Grow up. All this time on the road, are you fucking around?"

"A little bit but she doesn't know it."

"Myrna, Myrna!" Myrna emerged from the toilet in a pink satin robe. "Myrna, you should listen to this jerkoff kid I raised." Myrna shrugged and went back to the toilet. Warlock's dad drank deeply from his schnapps on the rocks. "Fran Tarkenton should come out of retirement. Bud Grant don't know shit from shinola."

Not a week later in early May Warlock was sitting in a Lake Leelanau tavern named Dick's Pour House. There was a lump of sadness in his throat over an unusual January memory: he had thrown a snowball at a big blue jay that had been bullying the chickadees away from the bird feeder. Warlock had knocked the blue jay into the bird version of eternity and wished he hadn't. He turned to greet someone tapping his shoulder: it was a grease-stained mechanic smelling of gasoline and oil. The man rubbed his filthy hands through his graying hair.

"Schmidt's the name. We're all set up. It turns out Feingold had nothing to do with it. It was an older partner whom we're luring up here whenever you want. Presented with the evidence it's my bet that both he and Rabun will pony up. Their option is a five to seven and they're both old. You owe me nine grand, including expenses."

"You want it in cash?" said the shocked Warlock.

"Of course I want it in cash, no bigger than twenties please."

"You sure would have me fooled." Warlock felt a growing admiration.

"I've never met anyone I couldn't fool. Even myself. Right now I got the feeling I could fix a car."

"Let's do it tomorrow," Warlock said, on a sudden impulse, and wanting to be shut of everything.

"Fine by me. I'm going to have to hook you for another few grand to set up the sucker shot in style. And by the way, I wasn't sure I should tell you this, but I've been tapping Rabun's phone and he's lunching with your wife tomorrow on a boat. Sorry."

"Thanks a lot." The wearing of invisible horns had to be the dreariest experience of his life.

44

It was not so much the boredom as the cold. It was past noon in early May with the wind, a northwester, sweeping down the arm of West Bay. There was a slight chop in the marina but beyond the breakwater there were five to seven footers, full of pale green furious water and foam, sweeping straight out ahead of the crests. This was purportedly spring but the wind was from the icy reaches of Manitoba, roaring down across Lake Superior, across the pine and swamp barrens of the Upper Peninsula, across Lake Michigan, until the wind hurtled itself against the bay town of Traverse City.

Warlock leaned against a light pole behind the power plant. He glassed the marina and its madly flapping gale flag with Diana's Leitz Trinovid bird-watching binoculars, a Christmas gift from her parents. They were an expensive item and he tried to protect them from the first drops of slight but stinging rain, a responsible gesture, the irony of which was lost on him. He slid the binoculars under his trench coat and took a sip of whiskey from a flask he carried to counteract the bad weather. He stomped his feet in the mud to keep them warm, thinking that though Florida was overloaded with perverts, it did have sunshine as a counterbalance. He squinted at the fifty-three-foot Hinckley center cockpit ketch bobbing in its slip, another expensive toy for the good doctor. Warlock would not have known it was a Hinckley ketch without having asked a marina employee an hour before; this nonchalance about particulars had been a disadvantage in the past ten months. He would have bet a week's salary that Schmidt was another anonymous grease monkey, not a top operator.

O Diana, O Diana, O lovely D., how could you? Tears fought for an exit but were met by a strong stomach grumble. What an asshole he had been not to bring a sandwich when there were those leftovers: a rare, roasted tenderloin he had studded with slivers of garlic and cracked peppercorns. He had wondered if it would be their last meal together. In an unwitting act of sensitivity she had brought him a new edition of Kenneth Grahame's *The Wind in the Willows* with illustrations by Michael Hague, a favorite book from childhood. She had thought it might help counter his depression and, after dinner, had read to him on the couch with his head poised dangerously on her lap. He roared with laughter and sentimental pleasure. Even betrayed people, he thought, don't act betrayed all of the time.

He stomped his feet, then did a few scissor jumps to revive circulation. Far out in the bay a serious rain cloud was approaching: a huge, black cumulus, intact as a giant dirigible. Directly underneath the cloud it was raining hard. Warlock studied the cloud with a painter's eye and thought it looked a trifle too ornate, with the sun shooting through the rain and intermittently casting a light that was alternately silver and yellow on Marion Island.

O Diana, O crazed bitch, faithless sodomite, wavering again into the cassoulet at the Lavandou in New York City. Was hunger yet another aftereffect of hate? He imagined opening the casserole and seeing her in foreign embrace, a visual decal on the delicious mixture of preserved goose, lamb, sausages and white beans. Diana's face cast its lovely image against the dark cloud he was still staring at, his head gradually craning straight upward, when the cloud dumped buckets of water upon him. Oh jesus. He ran to the car with the pieces of the shotgun inside his Burberry bumping painfully against his side. The forepiece fell out and dropped to the mud. He bent to pick it up and blacked out for a second, falling to his knees with a hand stretched out to the car door. The brief seizure passed and he flicked off a bottle cap that had stuck to his muddy palm. Inside the car he whispered a prayer to the god of murder and wiped the mud from the forepiece. He assembled the 20-gauge Fox-Sterlingworth, locking in the barrels to the breech, and noting how the forepiece snapped on with a loud and satisfying clack. They wouldn't leave the ketch in a hard rain because it was a long walk to the parking lot. O Diana, take me to Toad Hall where I can live with my own kind. Didn't I finally pull down your Calvin Klein jeans last night, tears streaked with laughter instead of tear tears, and head home with gusto, unmindful in my lust if the tender thicket had owned a previous intruder? It takes a while for a fucking Subaru heater to crank up, he thought, reminding himself to write the manufacturer in old Nippon. How had he managed to go through a C-note in a New York sushi bar, and then that haunting trip to the Mudd Club with Garth? He turned on the wipers and viewed the ketch through two layers of glass, amused with the distortions.

Finally, through the metronomic whacks of the wipers, he saw Rabun's head emerge from the hatch, then Diana's. He was out of the car in a shot, and running in the crouched manner of the SWAT teams on TV, the shotgun barrels poking out the back of his trench coat like fatal exhaust pipes. Warlock caught them just at the edge of the gangplank holding two umbrellas.

"The jig is up," he screamed, having failed to prepare a more appropriate line.

Their mouths made little circles of horror, sucking at the cold, wet air in disbelief; eyes flickering from Warlock's face down to the shotgun and back.

"Johnny, we were just having lunch," Diana said in a timbrous whisper that somehow made itself heard above the wind shrieking through the rigging.

"What did you have, a hot dog, you scheming bitch?" He found his voice breaking precipitously close to sobs.

"See here, I have a very important meeting with my lawyers from Detroit." Rabun spoke with the crisp fascism that would follow him to his deathbed.

"Sure you have a meeting you old goat fucker, you piss-gummed maniac. Touch my wife! I got your meeting right here in my hand. It's with death, with *mortedella* as the Italians call it. On your knees, and turn around! Turn around, on your knees!"

"Johnny, please, I can explain everything." Diana's smile had become wan indeed.

"Turn around or I'll blow this old fuck's head off. I mean it!" He raised the shotgun and they knelt with some awkwardness, trying to separate their umbrellas. He couldn't help but note that his umbrage had taken on a certain civic player's banality; he fired two shots into the water, and tossed the gun in before the rippling shot pattern had subsided. Then he ran for it.

Warlock drove home as if pursued by demons, the hounds of hell, the police. No one much, however, was out and about that stormy day, and the incident went unnoticed except by the participants, and by the marina employee in his shack who decided he had heard two claps of thunder. Warlock swerved his way down rainy blacktops, the roads covered by broken branches, and the pale pastel, green leaves of May stripped by the wind. He reached home, ran in the door, and flopped on the bed with Hudley, aroused abruptly from a nap, barking in pursuit. He clutched the pillow to his face, moaned long and hard, and sucked his thumb for a moment for the first time in thirty years, having broken the habit at boy scout camp.

Oh jesus, have I gone too far? he wondered. Diana definitely was going to be pissed off. Then the phone rang and he leaped to answer. It must be Diana, he thought, but it was Schmidt.

"Where the fuck are you? We're all here and Rabun comes in the door in a huff because a madman employee shot at him. Was it you?"

"Maybe yes. Maybe no." Warlock in his frenzy had forgotten the meeting. "I've been on a tail and got burned. Go ahead and get started."

The meeting had become a piece of ordinary cake by the time Warlock arrived. A much saddened, though innocent, Feingold was there. Schmidt had brought along three elegantly dressed cronies, posing as a Florida lawyer, an upper echelon IRS man, a State Police detective. The senior partner of the law firm, Bob Arrowsmith, was red as a beet at Schmidt whose services he had frequently used.

"I made you, I can break you," Arrowsmith hissed.

"Tell it to someone who gives a fuck, Bobby. Just sign the papers or it's Jackson. We can keep this polite. No one has to lose a job or go to prison. No one has to know a thing. We're just giving some rich souls back their rightfully unearned money."

Arrowsmith signed his admission of guilt and the papers were passed to Rabun who appeared, oddly, quite bored with the proceedings. Feingold had assured him that his life-style and research could continue unhampered. He signed.

"You're fired," he muttered to Warlock.

"No shit, Tonto. Right now the Traverse City police are taking an ounce of cocaine out of your glove compartment. You'll never see daylight again." Warlock gestured to the window and then everyone in the room stumbled for a view of the parking lot. "Just joking," he said; there was a definite sense that he had denigrated the solemnity of the meeting.

On the way home, for he had nowhere else to go, he stopped for a takeout pizza at Little Richard's, Diana's infantile favorite dish. He pretended he didn't like pizza unless it was home-made, but it took an entire afternoon of work to come up with an inferior product. Perhaps he could use this dish to win back her favor. Rare, indeed, is a woman or man so sullied that they can't be rebaptized with a few drinks, a pizza, and a shower.

45

The marriage didn't immediately return to the Camelot of yore, but then it had never been the Camelot of yore in the first place; and even that lordly kingdom, suspended in the mist between myth and history, had been rife with adultery and violence, albeit of a more courtly quality. And he couldn't admit that he had been merely sent away to facilitate their adultery.

Diana's afternoon had not become less tough after her encounter with the violent paranoia of her husband. (Even if Warlock's suspicions were correct, was it correct to fire a gun in anger, or was it a better idea to reserve a passionless judgment until he had his nose rubbed more directly in the unholy coupling? Is it paranoid to turn a corner when a midget approaches, swinging a sword? Do you leave a bar when some crazed hick cranks up a chainsaw, or do you wait for an imaginary tree to grow up through the floor?) The gale had felled a number of large tree branches in the area, and two different yokels had suffered heart attacks cutting up the branches before the storm had even abated. Once again he was led to envision her straddling their hirsute chests, and thumping with her palms to bring them back into a kingdom of chainsaws, unemployment, snowmobiles, ragged children, yards full of abandoned cars; but back to life, after all.

"How old were they?" He put the pizza on the dresser so she wouldn't fail to notice it. She was packing hurriedly but with the usual ruthless efficiency.

"About your age. Overweight, violent men, no doubt paranoid drinkers, killers of birds and fish and deer." He was alarmed at her hysteria which he had never seen before.

"Are you going somewhere?" She responded to his question with a haymaker slap. He pretended she hadn't done so. "I hope you're not going away too long."

"You're going to a fucking psychiatrist or you'll never see me again," she screamed in his face.

"I'll go to the psychiatrist thirty-three times if you'll read the complete file on Doctor Rabun. It's only by my good graces that your golden-age paramour isn't going directly to prison."

She read the file and wept. She wept long and hard, refusing any consolation. He was alarmed and wandered around the house with a lump in his throat. He fetched a ten milligram Valium, a pitcher of Margaritas, and a joint of *sin semilla* marijuana Feingold had slipped him at the Holiday Inn. He sat down across the table from her, insensitively humming *High Noon*'s "Do Not Forsake Me O My Darling." Finally her trembling fingers reached for the Valium, then a Margarita, then she lit the joint, drawing on it strongly and staring at him with reddened eyes.

"Why didn't you let me know about all of this when you came home in December? You let me be a victim of a terrible pervert."

"I didn't know what to do. I had a few setbacks in Florida where I didn't exactly come out on top. I began to doubt myself and I was afraid of losing you for good."

"Darling, Johnny, it wasn't really totally what you think. We'll talk about it later. My head is whirling."

Both their heads whirled that night and they only touched the raw spots with delicacy, tangentially, knowing that nature avoids direct confrontation. His empathy and love for her was so great that he told her the complete story of Laura Fardel, wanting to lighten the load of her grief. Diana caromed off the kitchen walls with laughter.

"Oh dear Johnny, how could you be so gullible?" she said, collapsing back into her chair.

"I wouldn't say that you've exactly been Miss Hip, darling. Was it the Dolphin, numbers one through seven? I bet it was." Warlock was referring to the elaborate prosthetic device Rabun had invented, and which the doctor planned to market under the trade name Dolphin. Warlock had questioned a possible ambivalence about the device in the big Miami market, but Rabun was entirely ignorant on the subject of pro football.

"Well, if you must know . . ." There was a lovely blush rising. "And you'll badger me forever. And you've promised to go to the psychiatrist thirty-three times. I had great admiration for him and he needed to conduct final tests before sending the device into production. So I did it. You don't need any sick details."

"I guess not." His brain was soaring along at fifty knots with visions of his beloved in the laboratory stirrups. "He never did you by himself?"

"He might have once. We took a strange South American drug in the living room and I woke up without my clothes."

"Where was he when you woke up?"

"In the kitchen cooking dinner. Let's stop this, Johnny. It's meaningless."

He bridled his curiosity with strain, stopping short of asking her what Rabun had cooked that evening. There was a tinge of inappropriateness to that question, he thought, getting up to put the pizza in the oven to rewarm.

"Sometimes I think we midwesterners from the country are not on our toes, you know? We're a little too altruistic and gullible. I mean we're not dumb. . . ."

"The tapes," she whispered with alarm, "he made video-tapes for research. But I wore one of those black eye-masks." She slumped back into the chair with relief. "He gave me a set of seven of those toys in a leather case with my name mono-grammed on the outside. I think we should burn them."

"It might be stupid to burn something worth that much."

He turned the oven up to maximum bake, impatient for the pizza. It would be best to roust Rabun for the tapes to prevent the likely event of blackmail, and, knowing the man, the tapes might be of professional quality. Despite the mask, he would not like to see the fair Diana as a short subject in a porn theater, under one of those absurd titles such as *Women in Science.* He was leaning against the oven, lost in thought, when he noted the heat was having a strange effect on his pecker. They exchanged a deep, wordless smile.

Diana suffered a modest mental relapse during the rest of May and all of June, a relapse he felt poignantly, knowing that he was partly the cause. In her own mind she had fallen from a high place, an utter dupe: since her teens she had read biographies about Madame Curie, Einstein, Schweitzer, Bohr, Oppenheimer, articles about Pauling, Debakey, Shumway. Every month he failed to do so much as open her inscrutable copy of *Scientific American.* Now she felt that her reverence for genius had brought her to shame. He tried to be inventive in his attempts to help.

"Look at it this way. If you were in the arts you might have fallen for the great Gauguin or Picasso."

"But Rabun isn't Gauguin or Picasso. He's a Hugh Hefner of the sciences." Diana mentioned the name of the prominent feminists' bête noire.

Considering her own mental condition he was a little irked that she insisted he fulfill his psychiatric promises. The total bill came to sixteen hundred and fifty dollars for which he received a few interesting recipes, some good travel talk, the suggestion that there were some infantile characteristics in his psychological makeup, and the pointed advice that he should send his wife to medical school rather than continue bothering her about a child. Was she involved with the psychiatrist? The greatest disappointment in her life had been winning first runner-up to a Washtenaw County Puerto Rican in the medical scholarship competition. The psychiatrist also had some interesting ideas on the fact that whereas orgasm caused an immediate, temporary memory loss, it didn't matter because no one had more than a slightly reliable memory in the first place. He never would admit it to Diana but he felt much better after he completed his thirty-three lap time trials with the psychiatrist who, incidentally, thought Warlock hopeless and harmless.

On the first anniversary of his dream of the future, though

he didn't know it, they took an arduous walk along the Manis-
tee River. On her days off they had been taking long, irksome
nature walks at his insistence. He claimed he wanted to know
details about birds, trees and flowers, when he really wanted to
cure her depression. Nothing out in nature, it seemed, resembled anything in the guidebooks. All of it did to Diana, but
perhaps she was faking it, he thought. At least these walks built
up a good appetite.

One mid morning they sat on stumps facing each other and
sharing the contents of his old boy scout canteen —a tepid
Chablis tasting acridly of tin.

"You have to go to medical school."

"Did the shrink say that?"

"Absolutely not. It's my idea and I insist. I'll visit on week-
ends. Don't forget I'm rich as Croesus." Who was Croesus?
The money had been coming in from Gloria and Ted Rabun
and Feingold hadn't stopped sending him Dr. Rabun's check
because he said he hadn't been "told to." "Promise you'll go
to medical school or I'll abandon you out here."

"I promise. It would be chicken of me not to try it."

They embraced tenderly halfway between their stumps.
Schmidt had called that morning trying to get him to chase
down some rich kid who had turned Moony. He had told
Schmidt he would only accept major assignments. Was the
Moony girl pretty? Diana's neck was damp and musky from the
walk. Over her shoulder there was a tingle of seeing something
move in the brush, but it was only Hudley. An idea entered his
mind that nature walks would be more interesting if there were
mythological guidebooks and you could find Toad and the
great god Pan out in the forest. With a few mutually exciting
movements they found themselves making love over Diana's

stump, deaf to the dog's bark. At the point of finishing it began to sprinkle. Was nature herself ever in confluence with man's wishes? There was a brief, light quarrel about where the car was, and they started off in opposite directions, promising to beep for each other. Ever the unfaithful friend, Hudley chose to go with Diana, his protector against the lightning and thunder.

Warlock's feet were light, his legs like steel springs as he ran through the wet forest. Perhaps deer watched with envy. Or not. He came to a dark swamp and looked up to watch a marvelous display of lightning. When the last shudder of thunder subsided he heard a strange bird; Pan piping, or a beep? He began to move into the swamp for no sensible reason, then paused letting his heart and breath calm. Then the beep came again, this time long and clear. There was no real reason to doubt it, he thought, turning around.